The Corsican Brothers

The Corsican Brothers

Alexandre Dumas

Translated by Andrew Brown

ET REMOTISSIMA PROPE

Hesperus Classics

Hesperus Classics
Published by Hesperus Press Limited
4 Rickett Street, London sw6 1ru
www.hesperuspress.com

*The Corsican Brother*s first published in French as *Les Frères Corses* in 1844
This translation first published by Hesperus Press Limited, 2007

Introduction and English Language Translation © Andrew Brown, 2007
Foreword © Frank Wynne, 2007

isbn: 1-84391-165-5
isbn13: 978-1-84391-165-4

CONTENTS

FOREWORD

'I spend much of my time among the dead and some of it with exiles,' Alexandre Dumas wrote.[1] 'I try to breathe life into long-dead societies, vanished men… who clashed with swords rather than brawling with their fists.' If the themes of death and exile, honour and betrayal, past and present run like intertwined threads through Dumas's novels of work, they find their first, eloquent expression in *The Corsican Brothers*.

Honour and betrayal might be said to have been his birthright. His father, the bastard son of Alexandre-Antoine Davy de la Pailleterie, a French marquis, and his black slave, Louise Dumas, had known glory in the army of Napoleon. In less than two years, the man they called 'the black devil' rose from the rank of lieutenant to become one of Bonaparte's most brilliant and valued generals by the age of thirty-one. But after their successful campaign in Egypt, Thomas-Alexandre Dumas dared to question Bonaparte's imperial ambitions, and requested leave to return to France. For his temerity, he was branded mutinous and found himself a virtual exile. By 1802, when his son Alexandre was born in Villers-Cotterêts, he was a walking shadow: half-crippled, deaf in one ear, and penniless. Alexandre, a child of the revolution – as attested by his birth date, 10th Thermidor, Year x[2] – barely knew his father who died when he was four years old; but he was to nurture the legend of his father's valour and Napoleon's perfidy for more than fifty years before he set it down.

Denied a military pension, Dumas and his mother were forced to live with her parents, so the young Alexandre

1. *Les Mille et un Fantômes* (1849).
2. 24th July 1802.

grew up roaming the fields of Soissons and Crépy. From his mother, he learned to write in an elegant, cursive script, from local poachers to hunt, fence and shoot, and from Father Consiel, the local priest, a smattering of Latin. In 1822, when he left for Paris, he had no prospects, no money and little education, but he had immense ambition, a prodigious imagination and a love of theatre kindled by his boyhood friend Adolphe de Leuven with whom he would co-write his first one-act play.

In Paris, he found encouragement from Général Foy, his father's erstwhile comrade-in-arms, and the elegant copper-plate handwriting taught him by his mother secured him a position as copyist in the *secrétariat* of the duc d'Orléans – later King Louis-Philippe. He revelled in city life, spending his meagre stipend at the Comédie Française, reading Schiller and Goethe and beginning to fashion himself as a writer. Through a combination of audacity, effrontery and self-confidence, he succeeded in having his first serious play, *Christine*, accepted by the Théâtre-Français, though it was not performed. Dumas, unperturbed, dashed off a second in less than two months. On the day before the premiere of *Henri III et sa cour*, Dumas sought an audience with the duc d'Orléans himself and invited him to attend. His Grace politely declined as he was to dine with thirty princes and princesses. Undaunted, Dumas audaciously proposed, 'If you, sire, will advance the hour of your dinner, I will postpone the opening of my play, so that your august guests may have the opportunity of witnessing a very curious spectacle.'

By the time the curtain fell and the audience – led by the duc d'Orléans and his party – rose to applaud the author, the success of *Henri III et sa cour* was assured. It was, in the words of a contemporary, 'more than a success, it was a coronation'. The following morning, Dumas woke to find himself enthroned with Victor Hugo and Alfred de Vigny as one of the leading literary figures of his generation. In the decade and a half that followed, the man who dubbed himself 'the indefatigable writer' wrote more than fifty plays, numerous essays and a series of *Impressions de Voyage*. He lived extravagantly, some said immoderately, travelled widely, he was profligate, ostentatious and an inveterate *coureur de jupons*. Yet the true flowering of his literary career came when, almost forty, his thoughts turned to the novel. His prodigious imagination never flagged and his prolificacy was dazzling. In a single year – the year in which *The Corsican Brothers* was first published – Dumas (aided by his researcher Auguste Maquet) completed *The Three Musketeers, Twenty Years After, Le Vicomte de Bragelonne* and *The Count of Monte Cristo*. His œuvre would eventually run to almost three hundred volumes, causing his many enemies to dub him *Alexandre Dumas & Co: Novel Factory.*

All this, however, was yet to come when, in 1842, armed with a copy of Mérimée's *Colomba*, Dumas set sail from Livorno to visit Corsica[3] in search of a lost world of simple, noble virtues. When he returned, according to one biographer,[4] 'wearing a sombrero and dressed in a black velvet doublet slashed so as to show his silk shirt and in Spanish breeches slit open at the sides and embroidered in gay-coloured silk, he made a sensation in the streets; it was all quite simple – he had been hobnobbing with Corsican bandits in the brush.'

Dumas also brought home a tale he had been told of twin brothers linked by a psychic bond, which was to become *The Corsican Brothers*.

3. If indeed he did. There is much dispute as to the veracity of the 1853 *Causerie* and Dumas certainly lied extravagantly about his life.
4. J. Lucas-Dubretonby, translated by Maida Castelhun Darnton, 1928.

Unusually, Dumas is a central character in this novel, and the tale, like the *Impressions de Voyage* is recounted as though it were fact rather than fiction, something which added to its power and immediacy – though as in all his novels he uses history only as a nail on which to hang his fiction. Dumas brings to *The Corsican Brothers* the erudition of an avid reader, the eye of a travel writer and the pace and verve of the dramatist. Though he claims to know little of the island, he knows its great heroes Sampietro and Paoli, and is familiar with Anton Pietro Filippini's *Istoria di Corsica*; moreover, he intuitively understands the death-fixated fatalism of Corsican culture, from which emerges both the cyclical justice of the vendetta, and its monuments – the *mucchios* which mark the spot of each violent death. Here, in embryo, are the themes that will inform all Dumas's later novels: exile and loss, honour and betrayal. In the brothers Louis and Lucien de Franchi, he crafts the opposing virtues of past and present. Lucien is a noble savage 'as much a product of the island as the green oak and the rose-laurel'; his brother Louis has become a Parisian, who has traded the Corsican code of honour to study French law. Both are men of honour, but Lucien's sense of justice is feral and his striving to arbitrate to end a brutal vendetta is matched by his readiness to fight, while Louis is a man of words, untutored in the use of swords and guns. Their fates are intimately bound up with their disparate characters.

For more than a century *The Corsican Brothers* was one of Dumas's most popular works. It was adapted several times for the theatre in both Paris and London and in 1898, became the first of Dumas's novels adapted for the cinema – it has since been filmed more than a dozen times. If it has been over-shadowed by the sheer brio of his later novels, this has done it a great injustice. In its brevity, *The Corsican Brothers* displays a rare economy and tension, rarely are a sense of place or mood more eloquently evoked than here, where Dumas's dispassionate eye transforms this simple shard of narrative into a glittering stiletto.

– Frank Wynne, 2007

INTRODUCTION

The link between Siamese twins has been called 'the most intimate bond'. It would be difficult to think of a closer relationship than that between Abigail and Brittany Hensel, born in the American Midwest in 1990 as what the medical profession, in its dispassionate terminology, calls 'dicephalic conjoined twins'. They share much of their trunk, but have two spines rising from the pelvis, separate stomachs and hearts, and independent heads and brains. Despite their condition, the two girls have achieved the most extraordinary things, and their successful relationship would seem to justify their parents' decision against surgery that could have separated them, but at the cost of confining them to wheelchairs, and would indeed probably have led to one twin being sacrificed to the other. Abigail and Brittany have claimed repeatedly that they have no wish to be separated. (If at any stage they reverse this decision, the surgery that would be involved will pose even more enormous difficulties than when they were first born.) They have different personalities, and different tastes in clothes and food. They share a circulatory system, but have somewhat different propensities to illness – Brittany tends to suffer more coughs and colds than her sister. But as their mother, Patty, has noted, if Abby takes the medicine, Britty's ear infection will clear up. The girls' nervous systems are largely separate: tickle one down her side and, in general, the other will not giggle; and yet they learnt to coordinate their movements (they each control one arm and one leg) so that they were walking by the age of fifteen months. Now they can ride a bike and swim, as well as play volleyball, basketball, kickball, and the piano, and even drive a car. Scientists have speculated that the girls' completely separate brains have managed subconsciously to image the movements of the other twin's limbs, and thus coordinate with them, to a remarkable degree.

Dumas's tale of Siamese twins, *The Corsican Brothers*, may pale into insignificance in comparison with this true-life story. Louis and Lucien, admittedly, were separated early enough for them to be, although uncanny doubles of one another, fully autonomous bodies, one of whom (Louis) goes off to Paris to become a lawyer, while the other (Lucien) stays at home to be… a Corsican (which seems profession enough for him). But their initial conjoined state has left its psychic mark: tickle Louis and Lucien will probably not laugh; but when Louis in Paris suffers heartache over a love affair that goes wrong, Lucien, far away in Corsica, feels the pain.

This premise enables Dumas to explore some stock romantic themes – namely those of second sight, uncanny premonitions of death, exotic otherness (Corsica, family feuds, vendettas), and especially the double. '*Zwei Seelen wohnen, ach! in meiner Brust,*' lamented Goethe's Faust: 'two souls dwell, alas! in my breast'. (The cover of the issue of *Life* magazine that reported on the progress of the Hensel twins in September 1998 showed Brittany, who controls the left part of their body, kissing Abby: the caption reads 'One body, two souls'. It is tempting, though perhaps facile, to remark that Faust showed rather less stoicism in dealing with his metaphorical plight than did the twins in coping with their real one.) Dumas's Louis and Lucien have 'two souls' but, thanks to what was once 'one body', communicate telepathically – admittedly a privilege of their family, not just a result of their initial union. Dumas does not speculate on the deeper paradoxes inherent in his subject matter. What if both Louis and Lucien are lovesick at the same time? Will they feel double the pain? Will Louis be able to tell which physical symptoms in his body arise from his own amorous plight, and which from Lucien's? Why does pain seem telepathically more communicable than pleasure? And what is pain, anyway? Part of the duality of the human condition lies in our status as (conjoined? semi-autonomous? potentially separable?) bodies and minds. What feels pain when I prick my finger? My finger? My brain and nervous system? My mind? 'Me'? Not just 'me': a child who falls over starts to cry, and another child his age, playing nearby, may burst into tears too (out of what one psychological vocabulary calls 'transitivity', a fluid sense of self that means that pain is easily diffused from one young child to another). If it's a heavy tumble, any carer nearby will also experience pain (heightened pulse rate and blood pressure, sweaty palms, all the symptoms of anxiety). Pain even crosses the barrier between reality and fiction: we see Gloucester being blinded, and wince in horror, even though there is no Gloucester and nobody's vile jelly is really being extruded. The action-at-a-distance posited by Dumas is merely a heightened version of the sympathy that makes us human.

Unusually, Dumas (typically an epic or third-person story-teller) includes himself in this story, as its principal narrator. (Unusually, too, it seems to have been, insofar as these words are ever quite accurate, 'all his own work' – this arch-colla-borator, who relied so greatly on the labours of others to flesh out his stories, here worked alone.) This enables him to create the 'effect of the real': the story bears all the marks of being an eye-witness account, and Dumas also makes men-tion of real-life friends, journalists, pistol sellers, acrobats and other figures who would have been well known to Parisians of his own day. And, to add to the verisimilitude, he was already well known as a travel writer: by 1841, the date at which *The Corsican Brothers* is set, Dumas had travelled widely in France (especially Provence), Switzerland, Italy, Belgium and Germany, and he had written about them all. So his readers were probably prepared to take at face value the opening sentence of *The Corsican Brothers*: 'At around the beginning of March 1841, I was travelling through Corsica.' If so, they were – it seems – mistaken. Dumas almost certainly (according to Dumas scholar Claude Schopp in his 2007 edition of *Les Frères Corses*) did not tour Corsica in 1841 or 1842 or indeed at any other time before the novel was published; one single document, a letter of his apparently sent from Bastia in June 1835, suggests that he made a very brief excursion from Toulon to Bastia that summer. Otherwise, he relied to a large extent on Prosper Mérimée's *Colomba*. That aside, once we are aware that the 'effect of the real' is a fake or, to put it more politely, a carefully constructed illusion, we can enjoy the story as a story.

Of course, the preponderance of direct, vigorous dialogue in Dumas's story, and its sheer readability, meant that it has since spawned many 'doubles' (adaptations, translations). It was easily turned into a stage drama (by E. P. Basté and Count X. A. de Montépin), and an English version of this was first performed at the Princess's Theatre, London, in 1852, albeit with a more melodramatic final scene than Dumas's dry, but oddly poignant, ending. There was also, perhaps inevitably, a campy, comic version of this play, *The Corsican 'Bothers'* [sic]; *or, the Troublesome twins. An original burlesque extravaganza. Founded on a famous romantic drama*, by Henry James Byron.

Dumas's storyboard style of storytelling here has sometimes been called 'cinematographic' – hence the remarkable number of film versions: Claude Aziza has counted seventeen, including eight silent versions, one from 1917. Some of these versions – all more or less unfaithful to the original – foreground the melodramatic and suspense aspects of this tale of revenge, others the potential for a supernatural *frisson*: déjà-vu, precognition, telepathy… Curiously, hardly any of the adaptations seem to keep the names Dumas gave his characters – 'Lucien' and 'Louis' – despite their being similar names connoting a half-shared identity, as with (to Western ears) the names of Eng and Chang, the original Siamese twins showcased by Barnum and Bailey. And neither has Dumas's historical setting been treated as sacred. The 1962 Italian-language version, *I Fratelli Corsi*, directed by Anton Giulio Majano, set the story back in 1822 and traced the line of revenge back to a family massacre: more Mafioso in feel than Dumas's tale, which relies on the admittedly bloody consequences of a dead chicken. And the situation at the heart of Dumas's story lends itself, at least in the showbiz world, to comedy as much as tragedy: Cheech and Chong's *The Corsican Brothers* (1984) apparently sets the story back (in every sense) to an even earlier age – the plotline on the IMDb website enthuses: 'two brothers who can feel each others' pain and pleasure mess up the French revolution'. Perhaps Steve Martin, with his taste for metaphysical hi-jinks, could turn his talents to this story? (Perhaps he already has.)

The concise Dumas style leaves relatively little room for a detailed depiction of Corsican manners. (It was, again, Mérimée – or even, later on in the nineteenth century, Maupassant, in such stories as '*Une vendetta*' – who had the ethnographic eye for the peculiarities of this unFrench part of France, this 'ninety-sixth *département*' that seemed spiritually much closer to Naples or Catania than to Paris.) What, after all, was Corsica to the average nineteenth-century metropolitan French mind? Probably a vague conflation of two words: 'Napoleon', and 'vendetta'. It was the island from which Naboulione Buonaparte, as he still called himself in Revolutionary Paris, or 'the ogre of Corsica' as he was viewed by Louis XVIII in Dumas's *Count of Monte-Cristo*, emerged, a semi-foreigner who made himself *the* French general par excellence. It was also the half-civilised (but therefore alluringly exotic) place where tribal loyalties meant that family quarrels were usually settled by the thrust of a stiletto, or a shot from behind a hedge, rather than by recourse to the local magistrate – the (relatively) peaceful reconciliation between the Orlandis and the Colonas here is clearly the exception, not the rule.

The political doubleness of Corsica is alluded to on several occasions in Dumas. Corsica still today has a dual identity, two souls in one body, sometimes fighting, sometimes cooperating. The spate of bombings, assassination attempts and murders carried out by Corsican separatists in the 1970s and afterwards has died down more recently. In 2000, Lionel Jospin proposed a deal whereby greater autonomy for the island would mean an end to separatist violence, and the fostering of the Corsican language, Corsu. These plans were vetoed by the Gaullists, who feared that they would be the thin end of the wedge: Brittany might follow suit, then Alsace… Nicolas Sarkozy, Interior Minister in 2003, and Jean-Pierre Raffarin, Jospin's successor as Prime Minister, proposed the suppression of the two *départements* of Corsica and, again, greater independence for the island: these measures were narrowly rejected by a referendum of Corsican voters in July 2003. The Corsican language may be threatened by extinction, or it may, like other threatened languages, rally. Dumas did his bit for it by preserving the word *mucchio*. This, or rather *mucchju*, denotes the funerary heap of stones piled up over a dead body: a telling word in a story that hints at the imminent erosion, even back in the 1840s, of the Corsican way of life. Perhaps the word *mucchju* will stand as a symbol of language death as well as a memorial to the individual deaths in Dumas's tale? Whether the Corsican language survives is no doubt written in the stars, or so the Corsican fatalist Louis would probably have claimed: as the Corsican proverb has it, '*Nanzi ghjunta la so ora nè si nasci nè si mori*' – 'nobody is born or dies before their time'.

– Andrew Brown, 2007

Note on the text

I have used the text published by Editions de l'Aube (La Tour d'Aigues, 2006), with its preface by Katty Péraldi-Andréani; I have also consulted the edition by Claude Schopp (Paris: Gallimard, Folio classique, 2007).

The Corsican Brothers

'…There are more murders among us than anywhere else: but you will never find any base or vulgar motive for these crimes. We have, admittedly, many murderers. But not a single thief. … '

'…Why send gunpowder to some rascal who will use it to commit crimes? Were it not for the deplorable indulgence that everyone seems to have for these bandits, they would long ago have disappeared from Corsica. … And what did your bandit do, after all? What crime led him to take to the maquis?'

'Brandolaccio committed no crimes! He killed Giovan Opizzo, who had killed his father while he was in the army.'

– Prosper Mérimée, Colomba

My dear Mérimée,
    Allow me to borrow this epigraph from you, and to dedicate this book to you.
    With heartfelt good wishes,

– Alexandre Dumas

At around the beginning of March 1841, I was travelling through Corsica.

There's nothing more picturesque and nothing easier to arrange than a trip to Corsica: you board ship in Toulon; in twenty hours you're in Ajaccio, or, in twenty-four hours, in Bastia.

Here, you buy a horse or hire one: if you hire one, it costs you no more than five francs per day; if you buy one, you simply make a down payment of a hundred and fifty francs. And there is no need to laugh at these low prices; this horse, whether hired or bought, can – like the celebrated horse of the Gascon which leapt from the Pont Neuf into the Seine – achieve things that neither Prospero nor Nautilus, those heroes of the Chantilly and Champ de Mars racecourses, could achieve.[1]

He can manage paths where Balmat himself would have needed crampons, and cross bridges where Auriol would require a balancing pole.[2]

As for the traveller, he has merely to close his eyes and let his mount get on with it: the danger need not concern him.

It is worth adding that, with this horse – which can get everywhere – you can travel a good fifteen leagues a day, and he won't even need feeding or watering.

From time to time, when you stop to visit an old castle built by some noble lord (the hero and chieftain of some feudal legend), or to sketch an old tower erected by the Genoans, the horse will browse on a clump of grass, nibble the bark of a tree, or lick a mossy rock. The problem is resolved.

As for your accommodation each night, things are even simpler: the traveller arrives in a village, goes right down the main street, chooses the house that looks most suitable, and knocks on the door. A moment later, the master or mistress of the house appears at the threshold, invites the traveller to climb down from his steed, offers him half of whatever there is for supper, as well as his or her own bed if there is only the one, and, the next day, sees him to the door, thanking him for the favour the traveller has bestowed by choosing this place to stay.

As for any remuneration, there is, quite evidently, no question: the master of the house would regard the least word on this subject as an insult. If the house is kept by some young woman, you can offer her a scarf, from which she will make a picturesque headdress for herself when she goes to the festival at Calvi or Corte. If the domestic servant is male, he will gladly accept a stiletto, with which, should he meet his enemy, he can kill him.

Still, there is one thing you do need to ascertain – whether, as sometimes happens, the domestic servants are relatives of the master, less favoured by fortune than he, who render him domestic services in exchange for food, lodging, and one or two *piastres* per month.

Do not get the idea that masters who are served by their great-nephews or their cousins fifteen or twenty times removed are any the less well served. No, far from it. Corsica is a French *département*; Corsica is still far from being France.

As for thieves, you never hear of any – swarms of bandits, yes, but you mustn't confuse the former with the latter.

You can travel fearlessly to Ajaccio or Bastia with a bagful of gold hanging from your saddle tree, and you will have crossed the entire island without having run the least shadow of a danger; but don't go from Occana to Levaco if you have an enemy who has declared a vendetta against you; I wouldn't answer for your safety even though these places are only two leagues apart.

So, I was in Corsica, as I said, at the beginning of March. I was alone – Jadin[3] had stayed in Rome.

I had come from the isle of Elba; I had disembarked at Bastia; I had bought a horse at the abovementioned price.

I had visited Corte and Ajaccio, and was now travelling through the province of Sartène.

On that particular day, I was travelling from Sartène to Sullacaro.

It was a short journey, maybe ten leagues or so, counting the twists and turns in the road and the outcrop of the main mountain chain forming the backbone of the island, which I had to cross: so I had taken a guide, for fear of getting lost in the maquis.[4]

At around five o'clock, we reached the summit of the hill which overlooks both Olmeto and Sullacaro.

Here we halted for a while.

'Where does Your Lordship desire to stay?' asked the guide.

I looked down at the village, whose streets lay open to my gaze. It seemed practically deserted: just a few women appeared now and again in the streets, and they were hurrying along, casting glances all around them.

Since, by virtue of the established rules of hospitality which I have just mentioned, I had the choice between the hundred or hundred and twenty houses comprising the village, I looked for the dwelling that seemed to offer me the greatest likelihood of being comfortable, and my eyes came to rest on a square house, built like a fortress, with machicolations in front of the windows and above the door.

It was the first time I had seen these domestic fortifications; but also, it has to be said, the province of Sartène is the classic land of vendettas.

'Ah, I see!' said the guide, his eyes following the direction indicated by my hand, 'we are going to the home of Madame Savilia de Franchi. Well, well, Your Lordship has not made a bad choice, and clearly has some experience of these things.'

It's worth remembering that, in this ninety-sixth *département* of France, Italian is spoken constantly.

'But,' I asked, 'is there really no problem in my asking hospitality of a woman? If I have understood correctly, this house belongs to a woman.'

'Yes indeed,' he replied in some astonishment. 'But what problem does Your Lordship imagine there will be with that?'

'If the woman is young,' I replied, moved by a feeling of propriety, or perhaps, if truth be told, of Parisian vanity, 'doesn't a night spent under her roof risk compromising her?'

'Compromising her?' repeated the guide, obviously trying to work out the meaning of this word (I had Italianised it with the usual aplomb of us Frenchmen, when we venture to speak a foreign language).

'But of course!' I replied, starting to lose my patience. 'The woman in question is a widow, isn't she?'

'Yes, Excellency.'

'Well, will she put up a young man in her house?'

In 1841, I was thirty-six and a half years old,[5] and I still saw fit to call myself a young man.

'Put up a young man in her house?' repeated the guide. 'But what difference can it possibly make to her whether you're old or young?'

I saw I'd get nowhere with him if I continued to employ this line of questioning.

'And how old is Madame Savilia?' I asked.

'Forty or so.'

'Ah!' I said, still replying to my own thoughts, 'ah, that's fine. And she has children, I expect?'

'Two sons, two proud young men.'

'Will I be seeing them?'

'You'll see one of them, the one who lives with her.'

'And the other one?'

'The other one lives in Paris.'

'How old are they?'

'Twenty-one.'

'Both of them?'

'Yes, they're twins.'

'And what profession do they intend to follow?'

'The one in Paris is going to be a lawyer.'

'And the other one?'

'The other one is going to be a Corsican.'

'Aha!' I replied, finding the reply quite characteristic, although it had been uttered in the most natural tone of voice. 'Very well, let's go for the house of Madame Savilia de Franchi.'

And we set off on our way.

Ten minutes later, we entered the village.

Then I noticed something that I had not been able to see from the top of the mountain: every house was fortified like Mme Savilia's, not with machicolations, as the poverty of their properties meant that such fortifications were probably too expensive for them, but purely and simply with beams of wood reinforcing the interior of the windows, while leaving openings through which rifles could be aimed. Other windows were fortified with red bricks.

I asked my guide what these loopholes were called; he replied that they were *arrow slits*, from which I understood that Corsican vendettas predated the invention of firearms.

As we advanced down the streets, the village started to appear more and more profoundly lonely and melancholy.

Several houses appeared to have withstood sieges and were riddled with bullet holes.

From time to time, through the loopholes, we caught sight of the glimmer of a curious eye watching us go by, but it was impossible to make out whether this eye belonged to a woman or to a man.

We reached the house that I had pointed out to my guide, and which was indeed the biggest in the village.

There was one thing which struck me, however: while the house appeared to be fortified by the machicolations that I had noticed, this was not in fact the case – in other words, the windows had neither beams of wood, nor bricks, nor *arrow slits*, but simply panes of glass, that were protected at night-time by wooden shutters.

Admittedly, these shutters still bore traces that an observer's eye could not fail to recognise as bullet holes. But these holes were old, and obviously went back a good ten years or so.

No sooner had my guide knocked on the door than it opened – not timidly and hesitantly, but opened wide – and a valet appeared…

When I say a valet, that's not quite right, I should have said a man.

What makes a valet a valet is his livery, and the fellow who opened the door to us was simply wearing a velvet jacket with a pair of breeches of the same material, and leather gaiters. The breeches were tied at the waist by a multicoloured silk belt, out of which stuck the handle of a Spanish-style knife.

'My friend,' I said, 'is it indiscreet for a stranger who knows nobody in Sullacaro to ask for hospitality from your mistress?'

'No, of course not, Excellency,' he replied, 'the stranger honours the house in which he stays. Maria,' he continued, turning to a servant woman who had appeared behind him, 'inform Madame Savilia that it's a French traveller requesting hospitality.'

So saying, he came down the eight steps leading to the main entrance – they were as steep as the rungs of a ladder – and took my horse's bridle.

I dismounted.

'Your Excellency need not worry about a thing,' he said, 'all your luggage will be taken up to your room.'

So I took advantage of this gracious invitation to laziness, one of the most agreeable invitations a traveller ever hears.

I started to make my way swiftly up the aforementioned ladder and took a few steps into the interior.

At a turn in the corridor, I found myself facing a tall woman dressed in black.

I realised that this woman, between thirty-eight and forty years of age, and still attractive, was the mistress of the house, and I halted before her.

'Madame,' I said with a bow, 'you must think it very indiscreet of me, but local customs excuse me, and your servant's invitation authorises me.'

'The mother bids you welcome,' replied Mme de Franchi, 'and the son will soon bid you welcome too. From now on, Monsieur, the house belongs to you, so make use of it as if it were your own.'

'I am requesting your hospitality for just one night, Madame. Tomorrow morning, I leave at dawn.'

'You are free to do as you see fit, Monsieur. However, I hope that you will change your mind, and that we will have the honour of detaining you for somewhat longer.'

I bowed a second time.

'Maria,' continued Madame de Franchi, 'take this gentleman to Louis's room. Light a fire there immediately, and bring some hot water. I am sorry,' she said, turning back to me, as the servant girl made ready to follow her instructions, 'I know that the first thing a weary traveller needs is water and fire. Please follow that young woman, Monsieur. Ask her for whatever you require. We are having supper in an hour, and my son, who will be back by then, will thus have the honour of requesting your presence, if you are dressed and ready.'

'You will have to excuse my travelling clothes, Madame.'

'Yes, Monsieur,' she replied with a smile, 'but on condition that you, in turn, will excuse our rather rustic welcome.'

The servant girl was climbing the stairs.

I bowed one last time, and followed her.

The room was situated on the first storey and looked out over the rear; the windows opened onto a pretty garden filled with myrtles and oleanders, crossed lengthwise by a charming brook that flowed into the Tavaro.

At the far end, the view was limited by a sort of bay of pine trees so close to each other they gave the impression of a wall. As in almost all the rooms in Italian houses, the walls of this house were whitewashed and decorated with a few frescoes representing landscapes.

I immediately realised that I had been given this room – which belonged to the absent son – as it was the most comfortable in the house.

Then I felt a desire, as Maria lit my fire and prepared my water, to draw up an inventory of my room and, from the way it was furnished, form some idea of the personality of the man who lived in it.

No sooner said than done. I pivoted on my left heel, thus rotating around myself in such a way as to review, in turn, the different objects which surrounded me.

The furnishings were quite modern, which in this part of the island, which civilisation has not yet reached, betokened a quite rare degree of luxury. It comprised an iron bed, with three mattresses and a pillow, a sofa, four armchairs, six chairs, a double cabinet of books, and a desk; all this furniture was in mahogany and evidently came from the workshops of the finest cabinetmaker in Ajaccio.

The sofa, the armchairs and the chairs were covered with flower-patterned calico, and curtains of a similar material hung in front of the two windows and enveloped the bed.

I had reached this point in my inventory when Maria went out, allowing me to pursue my investigation a little further.

I opened the cabinet of books and found a collection of all our great poets there:

Corneille, Racine, Molière, La Fontaine, Ronsard, Victor Hugo and Lamartine.

Our moralists:

Montaigne, Pascal, La Bruyère.

Our historians:

Mézeray, Chateaubriand, Augustin Thierry.

Our scientists:

Cuvier, Beudant, Elie de Beaumont.[6]

Finally, a few volumes of novels, among which I greeted with a certain pride my own *Travel Impressions*.[7]

The keys were in the desk drawers; I opened one.

In it, I found fragments of a history of Corsica, a work on potential ways of abolishing the institution of the vendetta, some poetry in French, and some sonnets in Italian: all in manuscript. This was more than I needed, and I was presumptuous enough to believe that I had no need to take my research any further: from all this I could form an opinion on M. Louis de Franchi.

He must be a quiet, scholarly young man, and a supporter of French political reforms. At this point I realised why he had gone to Paris to qualify as a lawyer.

A whole civilised future clearly lay before him. I thought it all over as I dressed. My outfit, as I had told Mme de Franchi, although not without a certain picturesque quality, still needed a little indulgence.

It comprised a black velvet jacket, open at the sleeves, so that my arms would be able to breathe at the hottest times of the day: Spanish-style slashes allowed a striped silk shirt to emerge. I also had a pair of trousers, held up from the knee to the calves by Spanish gaiters slit on one side and embroidered in coloured silk, and a fedora that assumed any shape one wished to give it – especially that of a sombrero.

I had just put on this nondescript costume, which I recommend to travellers as one of the most comfortable I know, when my door opened, and the same man who had let me in appeared.

He had come to inform me that his young master, M. Lucien de Franchi, had just that moment arrived, and was requesting the honour, if I was free, to come and bid me welcome.

I replied that M. Lucien de Franchi's wish was my command, and that the honour would be all mine.

A moment later, I heard the sound of rapid footsteps, and found myself almost immediately in the presence of my host.

He was, as my guide had told me, a young man of twenty or twenty-one, with black hair and eyes and a sunburned complexion; although rather on the short side, he was a well-proportioned fellow.

In his haste to present me with his compliments, he had come upstairs just as he was, still in his riding clothes – a green cloth frock coat, to which a cartridge pouch tied round his belt gave a certain military appearance, a pair of grey cloth trousers lined on the inside with Russian leather, and boots with stirrups. A cap, like that worn by our light cavalry in Africa, completed the picture.

From one side of his cartridge pouch there dangled a leather flask, and from the other a pistol.

He was also holding an English carbine.

Despite my host's youth – his upper lip was barely darkened by the faint shadow of a moustache – I was struck by the air of independence and resolution in his whole person.

You could see that he was a man raised to face a life of material struggle, used to living in the midst of danger without fearing it (but also without underestimating it): serious because he is solitary, calm because he is strong.

In a single glance, he had taken it all in – my travel bag, my weapons, the clothes I had just taken off, and those that I was now wearing. His glance was rapid and sure, like that of any man whose life may depend on a single glance.

'Please excuse me for bothering you, Monsieur,' he said, 'but I have done so with the best intention – that of ensuring that there is nothing you need. Whenever I see a man arrive here from the continent, I cannot help but feel slightly anxious; we Corsicans are still so savage that if we show, to the French in particular, the old-fashioned hospitality that will soon be the only tradition we have conserved from our forefathers, we do so with a tremor of apprehension.'

'You are quite wrong to feel anxious, Monsieur,' I replied; 'it would be difficult to meet all a traveller's needs better than Madame de Franchi has done; indeed,' I continued, glancing round the apartment in my turn, 'this is no place to complain of the so-called savagery that you have so kindly and frankly referred to; and, if I could not see this admirable landscape from my windows, I might believe myself in a room on the Chaussée-d'Antin.'

'Yes,' replied the young man, 'that was something of an obsession for my poor brother Louis: he loved to live in proper French style, but I doubt that, when he leaves Paris, this poor parody of the civilisation that he will be leaving will suffice him as it did before his departure from here.'

'And has it been a long time since your brother left Corsica?' I asked the young man.

'Ten months ago, Monsieur.'

'Are you expecting him soon?'

'Oh, not for another three or four years.'

'That is a very long period of absence for two brothers who, I imagine, had never been apart before?'

'Yes, especially for two who loved each other as we did.'

'I imagine he will come to see you before he finishes his studies?'

'Probably: at least, that's what he promised.'

'At all events, there is nothing preventing *you* from paying *him* a visit?'

'No… but I never leave Corsica.'

In the tone of voice in which he replied, there was that love of one's native land that views the whole of the rest of the world with equal disdain. I smiled.

'It must seem strange to you,' he replied, smiling in turn, 'that a person does not wish to leave a country like ours. What do you expect? I'm a product of the island, as it were, like the green oak and the oleander; I need my atmosphere, imbued with the sweet smells of the sea and the scents wafting from the mountain; I need my torrents to cross, my rocks to climb, my forests to explore; I need space, I need liberty; if I were transported to a city, I imagine I'd die.'

'But what caused such a great psychological difference between yourself and your brother?'

'Especially since we have such a close physical resemblance – as you would add if you knew him.'

'Are you very like him?'

'So much so, that, when we were children, my father and mother were obliged to put a mark on our clothes in order to distinguish us.'

'And when you grew up?' I asked.

'As we grew up, our habits led to a slight difference in complexion, that's all. My brother was always indoors, always bent over his books and drawings, and he became pale, while I was always in the fresh air, dashing up hill and down dale, and so grew more sunburned.'

'I hope,' I told him, 'that you will enable me to see this difference for myself, by giving me any packages you would like me to take to Monsieur Louis de Franchi.'

'Certainly – I will be delighted if you will be so kind. But my apologies, I see that you have made more progress than I have in getting ready for supper, and in a quarter of an hour, we shall be sitting down to table.'

'Are you going to change just for me?'

'If that were the case, you would have only yourself to blame, since you have set me an example; but in any case, I am in riding clothes, and I need to change into the clothes of a mountain-dweller. After supper I have an errand to run, and my boots and spurs would get in the way.'

'So you're going out after supper?' I asked him.

'Yes,' he replied. 'I'm meeting someone…'

I smiled.

'Oh, not that kind of a meeting; it's a business meeting.'

'Do you think I'd presume to want to hear the details of your private life?'

'Why not? We should live in such a way that we can tell people everything we do. I've never had a mistress and I'll never have one. If my brother marries and has children, I'll probably never even get married. But if, on the other hand, he never takes a wife, I'll have to get married; but only so that our race doesn't die out. As I told you,' he added with a smile, 'I'm an authentic savage, and I came into the world a hundred years too late. But here I am still chattering like a jackdaw, and I'll never be ready in time for supper.'

'But we can continue the conversation,' I replied. 'Isn't your room opposite this one? Leave the door open and we can talk.'

'I've got a better idea; come to my room. I'll get changed in my bathroom in the meantime… You're a connoisseur of weapons, I gather; well, you can look at my collection; there are some that have a certain value – historical value, that is.'

4

I readily accepted, as I wished to compare the rooms of the two brothers. So I eagerly followed my host, who, opening the door to his apartment, passed ahead of me to show me the way.

This time, I felt as if I were entering a real arsenal.

All the furniture dated from the fifteenth and sixteenth centuries: the sculpted bed, its canopy supported by four twisting columns, was draped in green damask with golden flowers; the window curtains were of the same material; the walls were covered in Spanish leather, and, in all the gaps, the furniture was crowned with modern and gothic trophies of arms.

There was no mistaking the inclinations of the man who inhabited this room; they were every bit as bellicose as those of his brother were pacific.

'Well,' he said, stepping into his bathroom, 'here you are in the middle of three different centuries: take a look. I'm putting on my mountain clothes, as I told you – after supper, I have to go out.'

'And where, amid all these swords, arquebuses and daggers, are the historic weapons you mentioned?'

'There are three: let's take them in order. Look by the head of my bed, you'll find, hanging by itself, a dagger with a wide hand-guard; its pummel head acts as a seal.'

'I've found it. Well?'

'It's the dagger of Sampietro.'[8]

'The notorious Sampietro, the assassin of Vanina?'

'The assassin? No, the murderer.'

'It's the same thing, it seems to me.'

'In the rest of the world, maybe, but not here in Corsica.'

'And is this dagger authentic?'

'Take a look! It bears the arms of Sampietro, but the French fleur-de-lis isn't on it yet; as you know, Sampietro was authorised to include the fleur-de-lis on his blazon only after the siege of Perpignan.'

'No, that was a detail I didn't know. And how did this dagger come into your possession?'

'Oh, it's been in the family for three hundred years. It was given to a certain Napoleone de Franchi by Sampietro himself.'

'Do you know what the occasion was?'

'Yes. Sampietro and my ancestor fell into a Genoan ambush and defended themselves like lions; Sampietro's helmet came off, and a Genoan on horseback was about to dash him down with his mace, when my ancestor Napoleone plunged his dagger into him, just where there was a chink in his armour. The knight realised he was wounded, spurred on his horse and fled, bearing Napoleone's dagger with him – it was so deeply embedded in the wound that Napoleone had been unable to pull it out. Now, as my ancestor was apparently very fond of this dagger, and regretted its loss, Sampietro gave him his own. Napoleone did not lose out in the exchange – this dagger is of Spanish manufacture, as you can see, and can pierce two five-franc coins placed one on top of another.'

'May I try?'

'Please do.'

I placed two five-franc coins on the floorboards and immediately plunged the dagger straight into them.

Lucien had been quite right.

When I took the dagger up again, the two coins were fixed to its point, pierced right through.

'Very well,' I said. 'It is indeed Sampietro's dagger. The only thing that surprises me is that, with a weapon like this, he used a piece of rope to kill his wife.'

'He didn't have the dagger any more – he'd given it to my ancestor.'

'True.'

'Sampietro was over sixty when he came back from Constantinople to Aix with the sole aim of teaching this great lesson to the world: women should not meddle in affairs of state.'

I bowed in agreement and put the dagger back.

'And now,' I said to Lucien, who was still dressing, 'I've put Sampietro's dagger back on its nail; let's move on to the next item.'

'You see two portraits next to each other?'

'Yes, Paoli[9] and Napoleon.'

'Well, next to the portrait of Paoli there's a sword.'

'I see it.'

'It's his.'

'Paoli's sword! And just as authentic as Sampietro's dagger?'

'At least as authentic, since, like that dagger, it was given to one of my ancestors – not a male one, but a female.'

'One of your female ancestors?'

'Yes. You may have heard of her. During the War of Independence, she came to the tower of Sullacaro, accompanied by a young man.'

'No, tell me the story.'

'It's a very short one!'

'Never mind.'

'We don't have time to stay here chatting.'

'Go ahead.'

'Well, the woman and the young man in question presented themselves at the tower of Sullacaro, asking to speak with Paoli. But as Paoli was busy writing, they were refused entry and, when the woman persisted, the two sentries pushed her away. However Paoli, who had heard a noise, opened the door, and asked what had caused it.

'"I did," said the woman, "I wanted to talk to you."

'"And what have you come to tell me?"

'"I came to tell you that I used to have two sons. Yesterday I learned that the first had been killed in the defence of his native land, and I have come twenty leagues to bring you the second."'

'The story you're telling me is a scene from Spartan history. Yes, it's just like one,' I said. 'Who was that woman?'

'She was my ancestor. Paoli took off his sword and gave it to her.'

'Hmm, I rather like that way of apologising to a woman.'

'It was worthy of both of them, wasn't it?'

'And now what about this sabre?'

'It's the one that Bonaparte carried at the Battle of the Pyramids.'

'And it doubtless came into your family the same way as the dagger and the sword?'

'Absolutely. After the Battle, Bonaparte gave orders to my grandfather, an officer in the Guides, to take fifty or so men and charge a knot of Mamelukes who were still gathered round a wounded chieftain. My grandfather obeyed, scattered the Mamelukes and brought the chieftain to the First Consul. But when he tried to re-sheathe his sword, its blade had been so badly dented by the damasked steel of the Mamelukes that it refused to go back into the sheath. So my father threw away the now useless sabre and sheath; and when Bonaparte saw this, he gave him his own.'

'But,' said I, 'in your place, I would just as much have the sabre of my grandfather, however badly dented, as that of the General in Chief, even though it had been preserved intact.'

'Well, look closely and you'll see. The First Consul picked up the dented sword, set the diamond you can see into the hilt, and sent it to my family with the inscription you see on the blade.'

And indeed, between the two windows, sticking halfway out of the sheath into which it would no longer fit, hung the sabre, dented and bent, with this simple inscription:

Battle of the Pyramids, 21st July 1798

Just then, the same servant who had first let me in, and then come to inform me that his young master had arrived, re-appeared in the doorway.

'Excellency,' he said, addressing Lucien, 'Madame de Franchi wishes me to inform you that supper is served.'

'Thank you, Griffo,' replied the young man, 'tell my mother we are coming down.'

Just then he emerged from his bathroom dressed, as he had said, as a mountain-dweller, in other words with a full velvet jacket, breeches and gaiters; all he had kept of his other outfit was the cartridge pouch around his waist.

He found me busy looking at two carbines hanging opposite each other and both bearing this date engraved on the butt:

21st September 1819 – 11 o'clock in the morning

'What about these carbines?' I asked. 'Are they historic weapons too?'

'Yes,' he said, 'at least for us they are. The one is my father's.'

He paused.

'And the other?' I asked.

'And the other,' he laughed, 'the other is my mother's. But let's go down, as you know they're waiting for us.'

And, going ahead to lead the way, he motioned me to follow him.

5

I must confess that as I went down I kept thinking about Lucien's last words. 'That carbine there is my mother's.' This made me look even more attentively at Mme de Franchi than I had when I had first spoken with her.

On entering the dining room, her son respectfully kissed her hand, and she received this homage with all the dignity of a queen.

'I am sorry, Mother,' said Lucien. 'I fear I have kept you waiting.'

'At all events, the fault is mine, Madame,' I said with a bow. 'Monsieur Lucien has been telling me and showing me such unusual things that my endless questions about them delayed him.'

'Do not worry,' she told me; 'I have only just come down myself; but,' she continued, addressing her son, 'I was impatient to see you and hear your news of Louis.'

'Is your son unwell?' I asked Mme de Franchi.

'Lucien fears he is,' she said.

'Have you received a letter from your brother?' I asked.

'No,' he said. 'And that's just why I'm worried.'

'But how do you know he is unwell?'

'Because, over the past few days, I have been unwell myself.'

'Forgive these everlasting questions, but that doesn't explain why...'

'Don't you know we're twins?'

'Yes I do – my guide told me.'

'Don't you know that, when we came into the world, we were still attached at the chest?'

'No, that I didn't know.'

'Well, it needed a scalpel to separate us; which means that, however far apart we may be nowadays, we still share a body, so that any impression, either physical or psychological, that one of us may feel has a corresponding effect on the other. Well, over the last few days, without any reason, I have felt gloomy, morose, depressed. I have felt painful contractions in the heart; it is clear to me that my brother is experiencing some deep sorrow.'

I gazed in astonishment at this young man who had told me such a strange thing without appearing to feel the slightest doubt. And his mother seemed to share the same conviction.

Mme de Franchi smiled sadly and said:

'Those far from us are in the hands of God. The main thing is that you are sure he is still alive.'

'If he were dead,' said Lucien tranquilly, 'I would have seen him again.'

'And you would have told me, wouldn't you, my son?'

'Oh, straight away, I swear it, Mother.'

'Good… I am sorry, Monsieur,' she said, turning back to me, 'but I have not been able to suppress my maternal anxiety even in your presence. Not only are Louis and Lucien my sons, but they are also the last of our name… Please sit here at my right… Lucien, sit there.'

And she indicated to the young man the vacant place on her left.

We sat at the end of a long table, at the opposite end of which six other places were laid for what in Corsica is known as the family, in other words those people who, in the main households, come between the masters and the domestic servants.

The table was copiously laden.

But I have to confess that, although I was just then filled with a consuming hunger, I contented myself with satisfying it materially, even though my mind was too preoccupied for me to savour any of the delicate pleasures of gastronomy. In fact, I had the impression that on entering this house, I had entered a foreign world, in which I was living as if in a dream.

So who could this woman be, who had a carbine as if she were a soldier?

And who could this brother be, who felt the same pains that his brother felt, three hundred leagues away?

And who could this mother be, who made her son swear that, if he saw her other son dead, he would tell her?

In all this, the reader will agree, I had ample food for thought.

However, as I realised that my continued silence was impolite, I looked up and shook my head, as if to shake off all these ideas.

Mother and son spotted straight away that I wanted to join in the conversation again.

'And so,' Lucien told me, as if he had been resuming an interrupted conversation, 'you decided to come to Corsica?'

'Yes, as you see: I had been nursing this plan for a long time, and I have finally realised it.'

'My word, you were right not to leave it too long; in a few years, given the way that French tastes and manners are flooding in so quickly, those who come here in search of Corsica won't be able to find it any more.'

'At all events,' I replied, 'if the old national spirit does retreat as civilisation advances and takes refuge in some corner of the island, it will certainly be in the province of Sartène and the valley of the Tavaro.'

'Do you think so?' the young man asked me with a smile.

'But it seems to me that what I have around me, in this very place, and right in front of my eyes, is a fine and noble picture of old Corsican manners.'

'True – and yet, though my brother had been living with my mother and myself, amid four hundred years of memories, in this very house of battlements and machicolations, the spirit of France came looking for him, took him away from us, and transported him to Paris, from whence he will return home as a lawyer. He will live in Ajaccio instead of living in the house of his fathers; he will plead cases, if he has talent he may perhaps be appointed King's Attorney; then he will harass those poor devils who have *scalped someone*, as they say in these parts; he will confuse the assassin with the murderer, as you did just now; he will, in the name of the law, ask for the heads of those who have done what their fathers regarded as a dishonour not to do; he will replace the judgement of God with the judgement of men and, in the evenings, when he has recruited a head for the executioner to cut off, he will think he has served his country, and contributed his own stone to the building of the temple of civilisation… as our Prefect puts it… Oh my God! my God!'

And the young man raised his eyes to the heavens as Hannibal must have done after the Battle of Zama.[10]

'But,' I replied to him, 'you can see perfectly well that God wanted to even things out: while making your brother into a supporter of the new principles, he has made you a follower of the old customs.'

'Yes, but who's to say that my brother won't follow the example of his uncle instead of mine? And then there's me – don't I sometimes allow myself to descend to things unworthy of a de Franchi?'

'You?' I exclaimed in surprise.

'Good Lord, yes! Yes, there's me. Shall I tell you what you have come to seek in the province of Sartène?'

'Tell me.'

'You have come with all the curiosity of a man of the world, an artist or a poet: I don't know which of these you are, and I won't ask you; you can tell us when you leave, if you like; otherwise you are our guest and need say nothing: you are perfectly free... Well, you have come in the hope of seeing some village in a state of vendetta, of being introduced to some noteworthy bandit of the kind depicted by Monsieur Mérimée in *Colomba*.'[11]

'Well, it seems I've come to a pretty good place for that,' I replied. 'Either my eyes have deceived me, or your house is the only one in the village that isn't fortified.'

'And this proves that I too am a degenerate; my father, my grandfather, any of my ancestors would have taken sides with one or other of the two factions that have divided the village between them for the last ten years. Well, do you know that I too find myself in the middle of it all, in the middle of rifle shots, stiletto attacks, knife thrusts? I'm the arbitrator. You came to the province of Sartène to see bandits, didn't you? Well, come with me this evening, I'll show you one.'

'Oh – are you really going to let me come with you?'

'Good Lord, yes, if it will amuse you, it's entirely up to you.'

'Well, I'm happy to accept. It will be a pleasure.'

'Our guest is quite tired,' said Mme de Franchi, glancing at her son as if she shared the shame he felt on seeing how greatly Corsica had degenerated.

'No, Mother, no, he really must come; and when, in some Parisian salon, people speak in Monsieur's presence of those terrible vendettas and those implacable Corsican bandits who still strike fear into the hearts of little children in Bastia and Ajaccio, at least he'll be able to shrug and tell them how things really are.'

'But what was the reason for that huge quarrel? To judge from what you have told me, it's now dying down.'

'Oh!' said Lucien, 'in a quarrel, it's not the reason that's of any consequence, but the result. If a fly happens to fly sideways and so cause a man's death, there's still one man dead as a result.'

I saw that he himself was hesitating to tell me the cause of the terrible war that, for ten years, had been laying waste to the village of Sullacaro.

But, as the reader will readily understand, the more discreet he became, the more I insisted.

'But look, this quarrel must have had a reason,' I said. 'Is the reason a secret?'

'Good God, no! It started up between the Orlandis and the Colonas.'

'What occasioned it?'

'Well, a hen escaped from the Orlandi farmyard and flew into the Colonas'. The Orlandis went round for their hen; the Colonas maintained that it was theirs; the Orlandis threatened the Colonas that they would drag them to the justice of the peace and make them swear an affidavit. Then the old mother, who was holding the hen, wrung its neck and threw it at her neighbour's face, saying to her, "Well, since it's yours, eat it!" Then an Orlandi picked up the hen by its feet and made to swing it into the face of the woman who'd thrown it at his sister's face. But just as he was raising his hand, a Colona who, as fate would have it, was carrying his loaded rifle with him, shot him point blank and killed him.'

'And how many lives did the ensuing brawl cost?'

'There were nine people killed.'

'And all that for a wretched hen worth twelve *sous*.'

'Indeed; but, as I was saying just now, it's not the cause, it's the result you need to look at.'

'And because there were nine people killed, there has to be a tenth?'

'Obviously not,' said Lucien. 'I'm arbitrating between them.'

'I imagine one of the families has asked you to do so?'

'Oh, good Lord, no; it was my brother who did so. They spoke to him about it when he was at the Lord Chancellor's. I ask you: do people in Paris really need to stick their noses into what happens in a wretched village in Corsica? It was the Prefect who did the dirty on us – he wrote to Paris to say that, if I would just say a word or two, there'd be a happy ending like in a vaudeville, with a wedding and a nice little song for the audience; then they must have turned to my brother, who took affairs in hand and wrote to me to say that he'd given his word for me. What do you expect?' added the young man, lifting his head. 'Nobody in Paris was going to get away with saying that a de Franchi had pledged his brother's word of honour and that his brother had not honoured the pledge.'

'So you have sorted everything out?'

'I'm afraid so!'

'And this evening we are going to see the leader of one of these two parties, I imagine?'

'Indeed; last night I went to see the other.'

'And is it an Orlandi or a Colona that we shall be visiting?'

'An Orlandi.'

'Is the meeting far from here?'

'In the ruins of the castle of Vicentello d'Istria.'

'Oh yes, I remember!… I was told that those ruins were nearby.'

'About one league away.'

'So we'll be there in three quarters of an hour.'

'Three quarters of an hour at most.'

'Lucien,' said Mme de Franchi, 'bear in mind that you're talking of yourself. You're a man of the mountains, you need barely three quarters of an hour; but our guest will not be able to manage the same paths that you can.'

'That's true: we'll need at least an hour and a half.'

'So there is no time to lose,' said Mme de Franchi, glancing at the clock.

'Mother,' said Lucien, 'would you mind if we left you now?'

She held out her hand to him, and the young man kissed it with the same respect as he had done on arriving.

'If, however,' added Lucien, 'you prefer to finish your supper in all tranquillity, then to go back to your room and warm your feet as you smoke a cigar…'

'No, not at all!' I cried. 'Devil take you – you promised me a bandit, and that's just what I must have.'

'Very well, let's get our rifles and set off!'

I bade a respectful farewell to Mme de Franchi, and we went out, preceded by Griffo, who lit the way for us.

Our preparations did not take any great length of time.

I put on a travelling belt that I had sent for before leaving Paris. From it there hung a kind of hunting knife, and it also contained my gunpowder on one side, and on the other side my lead shot.

As for Lucien, he reappeared with his cartridge pouch, a two-bore Manton rifle, and a pointed cap, a masterpiece of embroidery handmade by some Penelope of Sullacaro.

'Shall I come with you, Your Excellency?' asked Griffo.

'No, there's no point,' replied Lucien; 'just release Diamante; he might start a pheasant, and with the moon shining this brightly, we could do some shooting just as easily as if it were broad daylight.'

A moment later, a huge spaniel started bounding up and down around us, barking joyfully.

We walked a few steps away from the house.

'By the way,' said Lucien, turning round, 'inform them in the village that, if a few rifle shots happen to be heard in the mountains, it will be us firing.'

'You can be assured I will, Your Excellency.'

'Without this precaution,' continued Lucien, 'they might think that hostilities had resumed, and we would hear the echo of our rifles resounding in the streets of Sullacaro.' We took a few more steps and then went up a small alley on our right that led directly to the mountain.

6

Although we were only just at the beginning of March, the weather was magnificent, and might have been described as warm, had it not been for a delightful breeze that not only refreshed us, but also brought with it the pungent and invigorating odour of the sea.

The moon was rising, white and shining, behind Mount Cagna, and seemed to be pouring cascades of light out onto the western slopes that divide Corsica in two, and to some extent turn a single island into two different countries that are forever at war with one another, or at least are filled with hatred for one another.

As we continued to climb, and as the gorges down which the Tavaro flows plunged into the darkness of night impenetrable to the eye, we could see the calm Mediterranean looking like a vast mirror of burnished steel stretching out to the horizon.

Certain noises characteristic of night-time (because during the daytime they are drowned out by other noises, or else because they only really awaken with the fall of the dark) could now be heard. They produced, not on Lucien, who was familiar with them and could recognise them, but on myself, to whom they were foreign, strange and novel sensations that kept my mind continually on the alert, a state in which everything that one sees appears intensely interesting.

On arriving at a fork in the road, from which led two paths, one apparently skirting the mountain and one a barely visible track heading straight up it, Lucien halted.

'Now,' he said, 'are you sure-footed in the mountains?'

'Sure-footed, yes, but not sure-sighted.'

'You mean you suffer from vertigo?'

'Yes; I am irresistibly drawn to the void.'

'So we can follow this track. We won't need to confront any precipices, just some rather rough terrain.'

'Oh, I can cope with rough terrain all right.'

'So let's take the track, it will save us three-quarters of an hour's walk.'

'The track it is.'

Lucien went ahead, through a thicket of green oaks into which I followed him.

Diamante was trotting thirty yards or so ahead of us, combing the wood from right to left and, from time to time, coming back along the track, wagging his tail merrily to inform us that we could continue on our route without any danger, trusting in his instincts.

It was easy to see that Diamante was like the horses of the half-fashionable men of our day who work in the bank in the morning and are then society lions in the evening, and need a mount both to ride and to pull a cabriolet; he was trained to hunt both the biped and the quadruped, the bandit and the boar.

So as not to seem altogether ignorant of Corsican manners, I shared my observation with Lucien.

'You're wrong,' he said; 'Diamante does indeed hunt both animals and men, but the men he hunts are not bandits, but those that belong to that threefold race: the gendarme, the anti-bandit soldier, and the volunteer.'

'Oh?' I replied. 'You mean Diamante is a bandit's dog?'

'As you say. Diamante used to belong to an Orlandi, who lived in the countryside – I used to send him bread, gunpowder, bullets, in fact pretty much everything a bandit needs. He was killed by a Colona, and the next day they brought me his dog who was used to coming to my home and easily made friends with me.'

'But if I remember rightly,' I said, 'when I was in my room, or rather yours, I spotted another dog as well as Diamante?'

'Oh, that one – that's Brusco; he has the same qualities as our friend here, but he comes to me from a Colona who was killed by an Orlandi. As a result, whenever I go to visit a Colona, I take Brusco, and when, on the other hand, I have business with an Orlandi, I take Diamante. If anyone is so unfortunate as to unleash the two dogs at the same time, they devour each other. So,' laughed Lucien, his mouth twisted in a bitter smile, 'men can patch up their differences and make peace, they can take communion from the same blessed host, but dogs will never eat from the same bowl.'

'That may be just as well,' I replied in turn, also laughing, 'they are two real Corsican dogs; but it strikes me that Diamante, like all modest creatures, is evading our praise; ever since we started talking about him, he's slipped out of sight.'

'Oh, don't let that worry you!' said Lucien. 'I know where he is.'

'And where is he, if you don't mind me asking?'

'He's at the *Mucchio*.'

I was just about to venture another question, at the risk of wearying Lucien, when a howl was heard, so dismal, so prolonged and so poignant that I shuddered and halted, seizing the young man by the arm.

'What's that?' I asked him.

'Nothing; it's Diamante weeping.'

'And what's he weeping for?'

'His master... Do you really think dogs are men, and forget those who have loved them?'

'Ah, I understand,' I said.

Diamante uttered a second howl, even more prolonged, dismal and poignant than the first.

'Yes,' I continued, 'his master has been killed, as you told me, and we are approaching the spot where he was killed.'

'Indeed, and Diamante has left us to go to the *Mucchio*.'

'So the *Mucchio* is the tomb?'

'Yes… it's the monument that every passer-by erects on the grave of a man who has been assassinated; they throw onto it a stone or a branch. As a result, instead of sinking, like other tombs, under the tread of that great leveller called Time, the victim's tomb continues to rise, symbolising the vengeance that must live on after him and eternally grow in the heart of his closest relatives.'

A third howl rang out, but this time it was so close to us that I could not repress a shiver, even though I was fully aware of the cause.

And indeed, on turning a bend in the path, I saw, some twenty or so paces ahead of us, the white glimmer of a heap of stones forming a pyramid four or five feet high. It was the *Mucchio*.

At the foot of this strange monument, Diamante was sitting, his neck stretched out, his jaws wide open. Lucien picked up a stone and, taking off his cap, approached the *Mucchio*.

I did the same, copying him in every respect.

Once he was near the pyramid, he broke off a branch of green oak, and threw first the stone and then the branch onto it; finally, he made a rapid sign of the cross with his thumb, a Corsican habit if ever there was one, and a habit that Napoleon himself involuntarily repeated in certain dark and difficult circumstances.

I imitated him completely.

Then we set off again, silent and pensive.

Diamante remained behind us.

After some ten minutes or so, we heard one last howl, and almost immediately Diamante, his head and his tail low, trotted past us, darted some fifty or so yards ahead of us, and resumed his office of scout.

7

Meanwhile we continued to advance, and, as Lucien had warned me, the path started to become steeper and steeper.

I slung my rifle across my shoulder, since I could see that I would soon be needing both my hands. As for my guide, he carried on walking with the same easy confidence, and did not seem even to notice the roughness of the terrain.

After a few minutes climbing up the rocks, and with the aid of creepers and roots, we reached a kind of platform dominated by several ruined walls. These ruins were those of the castle of Vicentello d'Istria, the goal of our trip.

After another five minutes' climb, even more steep and difficult than the first, Lucien reached the top terrace, held out his hand and pulled me up to him.

'Well now,' he said, 'you don't do so badly for a Parisian.'

'That's because the Parisian you've just helped to get to the top has already made several excursions of this kind.'

'True,' said Lucien with a laugh; 'you have a mountain near Paris, don't you – name of Montmartre?'

'Yes; but apart from Montmartre, which I don't deny is a mountain, I've climbed a few others too – Righi, Faulhorn, Gemmi, Vesuvius, Stromboli, Etna.'

'Oh! Well in that case, you're going to look down on me – I've never climbed anything but the Monte Rotondo. Anyway, here we are. Four centuries ago, my ancestors would have opened their door to you and said, "Welcome to our castle". Today their descendant is opening this breach in the wall and saying to you, "Welcome to our ruins".'

'So had that castle belonged to your family ever since the death of Vicentello d'Istria?' I asked, resuming the conversation where we had left off.

'No; but before his birth it was the home of the woman from whom we are all descended, the celebrated Savilia, widow of Lucien de Franchi.'

'Doesn't Filippini[12] tell a terrible story about that woman?'

'Yes… If it were daytime, you could still see from here the ruins of the castle of Valle; that is where the Lord of Giudice lived. He was as much hated as she was loved, and as ugly as she was beautiful. He fell in love with her, and since she was in no haste to respond to this love as he desired, he informed her that, if she refused to accept him as a husband within a given time, he would forcibly make off with her. Savilia pretended to yield and invited Giudice to come to dinner with her. Giudice was overjoyed and forgot that he had achieved this flattering result only with the aid of threats; he turned up at the appointed place, accompanied by only a few servants. The door was closed behind them and, five minutes later, Giudice was taken prisoner and locked away in a dungeon.'

I passed along the path he had indicated and found myself in a kind of square courtyard.

Through the gaps which time had opened up, the moon shed great pools of light on the ruin-strewn ground. All the other portions of the terrain were left in the shadow cast by the remaining wall.

Lucien pulled out his watch.

'Ah,' he said, 'we are twenty minutes early. Let's sit down; you must be tired.'

We sat down, or rather we lay on a grassy slope facing a big gap in the wall.

'But,' I said to my companion, 'I don't think you finished the story.'

'No,' continued Lucien. 'In fact, every morning and every evening, Savilia would go down into the dungeon next to the one in which Giudice was being held, and there, separated from him by nothing more than a grille, she would undress and display herself naked to the captive.'

' "Giudice," she would say, "how can a man as ugly as you ever have believed he would possess all this?" '

'This torture lasted for three months and was repeated twice a day. But after three months, thanks to a chambermaid whom he had seduced, Giudice managed to escape. Then he returned with all his vassals, who were far more numerous than those of Savilia; he stormed the castle and, having in his turn captured Savilia, exposed her naked in a great iron cage at a crossroads in the forest called Bocca di Cilaccia; he himself offered the key of this cage to all those aroused by her beauty as they passed by: after three days of this public prostitution, Savilia was dead.'

'Well,' I remarked, 'it seems to me that your ancestors had a pretty good idea of vengeance, and their descendants, who go around killing and getting themselves killed with nothing more than a rifle shot or a dagger thrust, are mere degenerates in comparison.'

'Not to mention the possibility that they will stop killing each other completely. But at least,' the young man resumed, 'that's not how it happened in our family. Savilia's two sons, who were in Ajaccio under the guardianship of their uncle, were brought up as real Corsicans, and continued to wage war on the sons of Giudice. This war lasted four centuries, and did not finish – as you will have seen on the rifles belonging to my father and mother – until the 21st September 1819 at 11 a.m.'

'I do indeed remember the inscription, but I didn't have time to ask you to explain it to me; for, just as I had finished reading it, we went down to dinner.'

'Here is the explanation: of the Giudice family, only two brothers were still left in 1819; of the Franchi family, there remained only my father, who had married his cousin. Three months after this marriage, the Giudice brothers decided to have done with us once and for all. One of them laid an ambush on the Olmedo road and waited for my father who was on his way back from Sartène, while the other, profiting from this absence, was to storm our house. The plan was duly carried out, but turned out quite differently from what the attackers had expected. My father had been forewarned and was on his guard; my mother had also been informed and had assembled our shepherds, so that when this two-fold attack took place, everyone was ready to defend their respective places: my father on the mountain, my mother in my very room. After a fight lasting five minutes, the two brothers had fallen, the one struck down by my father and the other by my mother. On seeing his enemy fall, my father took out his watch: it was eleven o'clock! As she saw her adversary fall, my mother turned to look at the clock: it was eleven o'clock! The whole business had been concluded at the same minute: there were no more Giudices, their race had been destroyed. The Franchi family was victorious; they could now live in peace, and, since they had worthily fulfilled their task during this four-century-long war, they no longer took an active part in events; however, my father had the date and time of this strange turn of events inscribed on the butts of all the rifles that had been fired, and hung them on either side of the clock, at the same place where you saw them. Seven months later, my mother gave birth to two twins, one of whom is your humble servant, the Corsican, Lucien, and the other the philanthropist Louis, his brother.'

Just then, on one of the moonlit stretches of terrain, I saw the shadow of a man and that of a dog.

It was the shadow of the bandit Orlandi and that of our friend Diamante.

At the same time, we heard the chimes of the Sullacaro bell slowly tolling nine o'clock.

Master Orlandi apparently shared the opinion of Louis XV; as everyone knows, he held to the maxim that punctuality is the politeness of kings.

It would have been impossible to be more punctual than this king of the mountains, whom Lucien had requested to arrive at nine o'clock precisely.

On seeing him, we both rose to our feet.

8

'You are not alone, Monsieur Lucien?' said the bandit.

'Don't worry about that, Orlandi; this gentleman is a friend of mine who has heard about you and wanted to pay you a visit. I thought I couldn't refuse him this pleasure.'

'You are welcome to the countryside, Monsieur,' said the bandit with a bow, taking a few steps towards us.

I returned his greeting with the most punctilious politeness.

'You must have been here for some time already?' continued Orlandi.

'Yes, about twenty minutes.'

'Ah, that explains it: I heard Diamante howling at the *Mucchio*, and he came to join me a good quarter of an hour ago. He's a good, faithful beast, isn't he, Monsieur Lucien?'

'Yes, that's just how he is, Orlandi: good and faithful,' replied Lucien, stroking Diamante.

'But since you knew that Monsieur Lucien was there,' I asked, 'why didn't you come earlier?'

'Because we'd arranged to meet at nine o'clock,' replied the bandit, 'and it's just as lacking in punctuality to arrive a quarter of an hour early as to arrive a quarter of an hour late.'

'Is that a criticism of me, Orlandi?' asked Lucien with a laugh.

'No, Monsieur; *you* might well have had your reasons; anyway, you're in the countryside, and it's probably because of Monsieur that you broke with your usual habits; for you too are punctual, Monsieur Lucien, and I know that better than anyone; you have put yourself out for me quite a few times, thank God!'

'There is no need to thank me for that, Orlandi; this will probably be the last time.'

'Don't we have a few things to say to each other on that subject, Monsieur Lucien?' asked the bandit.

'Yes, and if you will follow me…'

'I am yours to command.'

Lucien turned to me.

'You will excuse me, I hope?' he said.

'But of course, please go ahead!'

They both moved away and, climbing onto the breach in the wall through which Orlandi had appeared, they stood there for a while, standing out clearly demarcated against the moonlight that seemed to bathe the outlines of their two dark silhouettes with a silver gleam.

Only then could I look more attentively at Orlandi.

He was a tall man with a full beard, dressed exactly the same way as the young de Franchi, apart from the fact that his clothes bore the trace of frequent contact with the maquis in which their wearer lived, the brambles through which he had on more than one occasion been forced to escape, and the earth on which he slept every night.

I couldn't hear what he was saying for two reasons: they were ten yards or so away from me, and they were speaking in Corsican dialect.

But I could easily see from their movements that the bandit was heatedly rejecting a series of arguments that the young man was setting forth with a calm that did honour to the impartiality he brought to this business.

Eventually, Orlandi's gestures became less frequent and more vigorous; his very words seemed to grow less vehement; at one final remark, he lowered his head; then, finally, after a moment, he held out his hand to the young man.

Their conference was in all probability over, since both of them came back to me.

'My dear guest,' the young man said to me, 'here is Orlandi; he wishes to shake your hand to thank you.'

'What for?' I asked.

'For agreeing to be one of his sponsors, of course. I promised that you would.'

'If you promised that I would, you will understand that I accept even without knowing what it's about.'

I held my hand out to the bandit, who did me the honour of touching it with his fingertips.

'In this way,' continued Lucien, 'you'll be able to tell my brother that everything has been arranged in accordance with his desires, and that you have even signed the contract.'

'So is there a wedding taking place?'

'No, not yet; but perhaps it will come.'

A smile of disdain passed across the lips of the bandit.

'Peace, yes,' he said, 'since you absolutely wish it, Monsieur Lucien, but no marriage: that isn't part of the treaty.'

'No,' said Lucien, 'it's merely written, in all probability, in the future. But let's talk about something else. You didn't hear anything while I was talking with Orlandi, did you?'

'You mean did I hear any of what you were saying?'

'No, of what a pheasant was saying nearby.'

'Actually, I did think I heard a mating cry; but I decided I must have misheard.'

'You hadn't misheard,' said Orlandi, 'there's a cock pheasant perched on the branch of the big chestnut tree, you know, Monsieur Lucien, a hundred paces from here. I heard it just now as we came by.'

'Well then!' said Lucien cheerfully, 'in that case we must have it for supper tomorrow.'

'It would already be down,' said Orlandi, 'if I hadn't been afraid that people in the village might think I was shooting at something other than a pheasant.'

'I forewarned them,' said Lucien. 'By the way,' he added, turning towards me and flinging his freshly loaded rifle across his shoulder, 'the honour is all yours.'

'Just a moment! I'm not as sure as you are of hitting my aim; and I'm really rather keen to eat my share of your pheasant: so *you* shoot it.'

'Indeed,' said Lucien, 'you're not as used as we are to hunting at night, and you'd certainly fire too low; in any case, if you don't have anything to do tomorrow, you can take your turn then.'

9

We left the ruins on the other side from that we had entered, with Lucien walking first.

Just as we were stepping out into the maquis, the pheasant gave its presence away by uttering its mating call again.

It was some eighty or so paces away from us, hidden in the branches of a chestnut tree which was protected on all sides by thick scrubland.

'How can you get up to it without it hearing you?' I asked Lucien. 'It doesn't strike me as very easy.'

'No,' he replied. 'If only I could see it, I'd shoot from here.'

'What, from here? Do you have a rifle that can kill pheasants at forty yards?'

'Not with lead shot; but with a bullet, yes.'

'Oh, a bullet! Say no more, that's quite different; and you were right to assume responsibility for taking the shot.'

'Do you want to see it?' asked Orlandi.

'Yes,' said Lucien, 'I have to admit I'd really like to.'

'Well, just wait.'

And Orlandi started to mimic the clucking of the pheasant hen.

At the same moment, without seeing the pheasant, we spotted movement in the branches of the chestnut tree: the pheasant was climbing up from branch to branch, while replying with its mating call to the advances Orlandi was making.

Finally it appeared at the top of the tree, perfectly visible, and standing out distinctly against the dull white of the sky.

Orlandi fell silent and the pheasant remained immobile.

At the same moment, Lucien lowered his rifle, and, after taking careful aim for a second, fired.

The pheasant fell like a pelota ball.

'Go get him!' said Lucien to Diamante.

The dog sped off into the maquis, and, five minutes later, returned with the pheasant in his jaws.

The bullet had gone straight through its body.

'Good shot,' I said. 'Allow me to congratulate you – especially with a double rifle.'

'Oh,' said Lucien, 'it was less difficult than you might think; one of the barrels is rifled and carries the bullet like a carbine.'

'All the same – even with a carbine the shot would still deserve applause.'

'Bah!' said Orlandi, 'with a carbine, Monsieur Lucien can hit a five-franc coin at a hundred and fifty yards.'

'And do you shoot a pistol as well as you do a rifle?'

'More or less, I suppose,' said Lucien; 'at twenty-five paces, I'll always slice six out of twelve bullets on the blade of a knife.'

I raised my hat and saluted Lucien.

'And what about your brother,' I asked, 'is he as good as you?'

'My brother?' he said. 'Poor Louis! He has never touched either a rifle or a pistol. So I am constantly afraid in case he ends up fighting a duel in Paris; he's a brave chap, and he'd get himself killed if it was a question of maintaining his country's honour.'

And Lucien pushed the pheasant into the pocket of his big velvet bag.

'Well now,' he said, 'my dear Orlandi, see you tomorrow.'

'See you tomorrow, Monsieur Lucien.'

'I know how punctual you are: at ten o'clock, you, your friends and relatives will all be at the end of the street, won't you? On the side near the mountain, at the same hour, and at the other end of the street, Colona will be there with his friends and relatives. As for us, we'll be on the church steps.'

'It's all arranged, Monsieur Lucien; thanks for taking the trouble. And as for you, Monsieur,' continued Orlandi, turning to me and saluting me, 'thank you for the honour.'

And, on this exchange of compliments, we went our separate ways, with Orlandi returning to the maquis, and us taking the road back to the village.

As for Diamante, he was unable for a moment to decide whether to follow Orlandi or us, gazing left and right in turn. After five minutes' hesitation, we were honoured to see that he preferred us.

I have to confess that I had felt a little anxious, while climbing the double wall of rocks that I mentioned before, as to how I would get down again; as everyone knows, coming down is generally much more difficult than going up.

I saw with some pleasure that Lucien, doubtless guessing what I was thinking, had chosen to follow a different path from the one we had come up.

This route gave me an added advantage, that of conversation, which was of course difficult to maintain when the going was steep.

Now, as the slope was gentle and the path easy, I had not gone thirty yards before I started asking my usual questions.

'So,' I said, 'peace has been restored?'

'Yes, and – as you saw – it wasn't easy. I finally got him to realise that all the advances had been made by the Colonas. First, they had had five men killed, while the Orlandis had had only four. The Colonas had agreed to the reconciliation yesterday, while the Orlandis agreed to it only today. Finally, the Colonas had committed themselves to surrendering a live hen to the Orlandis in public, a concession proving that they recognised they had been in the wrong. This last consideration swayed him.'

'And it's tomorrow that this touching reconciliation is due to take place?'

'Tomorrow at ten. You can see that you're not so unlucky after all. You'd been hoping to see a vendetta!'

The young man continued, laughing bitterly.

'Bah! A vendetta's a fine thing, but... In Corsica people have been talking about nothing else for the last four centuries. You're going to see a reconciliation. That's much rarer than a vendetta.'

I started to laugh.

'As you see,' he told me, 'you're laughing at us, and you're right to do so; we really are odd people.'

'No,' I said, 'I'm laughing at something strange – seeing you furious at yourself for having succeeded so well.'

'You're right! Ah, if you'd been able to understand what I was saying, you'd have admired my eloquence. But come back in ten years' time, and you can rest assured, all the people here will be talking French.'

'You're an excellent advocate.'

'No, let's get this clear: I'm an arbitrator. What the devil do you expect? The duty of an arbitrator is conciliation. If I were appointed as arbitrator between God and Satan, I'd try to bring them together, though in my heart of hearts I'm convinced that, if he took my advice, God might well do something silly.'

As I saw that this kind of conversation was merely souring my travelling companion's mood, I dropped the conversation, and as, for his part, he didn't try to resume it, we reached home without another word.

10

Griffo was waiting.

Before his master said anything to him, he rummaged in his jacket pocket and pulled out the pheasant. He had heard and recognised the rifle shot.

Madame de Franchi had still not gone to bed; she had just retired to her room, telling Griffo to ask her son to come and see her before he withdrew for the night.

The young man enquired whether there was anything I needed and, when I replied in the negative, asked me for permission to obey his mother's orders.

I gave him my full permission and went up to my room.

I felt a certain pride on seeing it again. My studies on analogies had not deceived me, and I congratulated myself on having guessed at Louis's character in the same way I would have guessed at Lucien's.

So I undressed slowly, and, after taking Victor Hugo's *Les Orientales* from the library of the future lawyer, I went to bed, filled with self-satisfaction.

I had just reread for the hundredth time the poem entitled '*Le Feu du ciel*'[13] when I heard footsteps coming up the stairs and stopping quietly outside my door; I guessed it was my host who had come to wish me goodnight, but was probably afraid I might already be asleep and was hesitating to open the door.

'Come in,' I said, placing my book on the bedside table.

And indeed, the door opened and Lucien appeared.

'Excuse me,' he said, 'but when I think back over it, it strikes me I was so glum this evening that I didn't want to go to bed without first coming to apologise to you; so I'm here to make honourable amends. And, as you still seem to have a number of questions to ask me, I am here at your entire disposal.'

'Thank you a hundred times over,' I said; 'you have been so obliging that, in fact, I am more or less well informed about everything I wished to know, and there is only one thing I still need to find out. And I promised myself that I wouldn't ask you that.'

'Why?'

'Because it really would be far too indiscreet. However, I can tell you now, don't press me; I might regret it.'

'Oh well, in that case, just ask away: an unsatisfied curiosity is a bad thing; it naturally arouses suppositions, and, out of three suppositions, there are always at least two which are more prejudicial to the man they concern than the truth would be.'

'You can rest assured on that point: my most injurious suppositions about you lead me simply to the conclusion that you are a sorcerer.'

The young man started to laugh.

'Devil take it!' he said. 'You are going to make me as curious as yourself; do speak out, I beg you.'

'Very well. You have been kind enough to elucidate everything that was obscure for me, except for one single point. You have shown me those fine weapons – I'll be asking for your permission to see them again before I leave.'

'One!'

'You have explained to me the meaning of that double (and similar) inscription on the butt of the two rifles.'

'Two!'

'You have enabled me to understand how, thanks to the phenomenon of your birth, you can feel, three hundred leagues away, the sensations felt by your brother, just as, on his side, he doubtless feels your sensations too.'

'Three!'

'But when Madame de Franchi mentioned how melancholy you felt – something that gives you the impression something bad has happened to your brother – and asked you whether you were sure he wasn't dead, you replied: "No, if he were dead, I would have seen him again".'

'Yes, it's true, that's what I said.'

'Well, if the explanation for those words may enter profane ears, please explain them to me.'

The young man's face had assumed, as I spoke, such a grave expression that I uttered the last words with some hesitation.

Indeed, after I had finished speaking, a moment of silence fell between the two of us.

'Look,' I said, 'I can see that was indiscreet of me; let's pretend I never said anything.'

'No,' he said; 'but you are a man of the world, and thus inclined to scepticism. Well, I do not want to see you treating as a superstition an ancient family tradition that has existed among us for four hundred years.'

'Listen,' I told him, 'I'll swear one thing to you. Nobody, when it comes to legends and traditions, is more credulous than I am, and there are even certain things in which I have a particular belief: impossible things.'

'So might you believe in apparitions?'

'Do you want me to tell you what once happened to me?'

'Yes, that will encourage me.'

'My father died in 1807, so, at that time, I was not yet three and a half.[14] As the doctor had announced that the patient was not long for this world, I had been taken to the home of an old female cousin who lived in our house between courtyard and garden.

'She had put a bed for me opposite hers, and tucked me up at my usual time. In spite of the misfortune hanging over me, of which I was not in any case aware, I had gone to sleep; all of a sudden, there were three violent bangs on the door of our bedroom; I woke up, climbed out of bed, and went over to the door.

'"Where are you going?" my cousin asked me.

'She had been woken up, as I had, by these three bangs, and could not conceal a certain terror, knowing as she did that – since the main door onto the street was closed – nobody could knock at the door of the room in which we were.

'"I'm going to open the door for Papa, he has come to bid me farewell," I replied.

'Then it was she who leapt out of bed and put me back in mine, in spite of my objections; I was weeping, and I kept shouting:

'"Papa is at the door, and I want to see Papa before he goes away for ever."'

'And since then, has the apparition ever returned?' asked Lucien.

'No, even though I have called for it to do so many times; but perhaps it is also true that God grants to a child's purity certain privileges that he refuses to a man's corruption.'

'Well,' said Lucien with a smile, 'in our family, we are more fortunate than you.'

'Do you see your dead relatives again?'

'Every time that some great event is about to occur or has occurred.'

'And to what do you attribute this privilege being granted to your family?'

'This is what has been preserved as a tradition among us: I told you that Savilia died leaving two sons.'

'Yes, I remember.'

'Those two sons grew, loving each other with all the love they would otherwise have directed towards their other relatives, if their other relatives had lived. So they swore to each other that nothing would ever be able to separate them, not even death; and, after uttering a powerful oath, they wrote in their blood, on a piece of parchment that they then divided between them, the mutual pledge that the first one to die would appear to the other, first at the time of his own death, and then at all the most significant moments of his life. Three months later, one of the two brothers was killed in an ambush, just as the other was sealing a letter meant for him; but, no sooner had he placed his seal on the still molten wax than he heard a sigh behind him, and, turning round, he saw his brother standing there with his hand on his shoulder, although he could not feel that hand. Then, mechanically, he held out to him the letter that was meant for him; the other man took the letter and disappeared. On the eve of his death, he saw him again. Doubtless the two brothers had not made this pledge just for themselves, but for their descendants too; for ever since that time, the apparitions have been repeated, not just at the moment of the death of those passing away, but also on the eve of all great events.'

'And have you ever seen any apparition?'

'No; but as my father was, on the night before his death, warned by his father that he was about to die, I presume that my brother and I will enjoy our ancestors' privilege, having done nothing to lose this favour.'

'And this privilege is granted only to the males of the family?'

'Yes.'

'Strange!'

'That's how it is.'

I gazed at this young man who was telling me, in his cold, grave, calm voice, of something regarded as impossible, and I repeated with Hamlet:

'There are more things in heaven and earth, Horatio,
Than are dreamt of in your philosophy.'

In Paris, I would have assumed that this young man was a hoaxer; but in the depths of Corsica, in a small, unknown village, one had quite simply to consider him either as a madman who was, in all honesty, deluded, or as a privileged being, happier or unhappier than other men.

'And now,' he said after a long silence, 'do you know everything that you want to know?'

'Yes, thank you,' I replied; 'I am touched by your trust in me, and I promise that I will keep your secret.'

'Oh, good Lord,' he said with a smile, 'there's no secret in it, and any peasant in the village would have told this story just as I am telling it to you; I merely hope that, in Paris, my brother has not boasted of this privilege, which would probably lead to the men laughing in his face, and to the women having attacks of the vapours.'

And on these words he arose and, wishing me goodnight, withdrew into his room.

Although tired, I found it rather difficult to get to sleep; and even when I did doze off, my sleep was troubled.

In my dream, I hazily saw all the people to whom I had been introduced during the day, but they were involved together in some confused and inconsequential action. Only at daybreak did I really get off to sleep, and I did not awaken until I heard the sound of the church bell that seemed to be chiming right in my ears.

I pulled the servant's bell, for my epicurean predecessor had indulged himself by having the pull-string of a small bell placed within reach – it was probably the only one that existed in the whole village.

Immediately Griffo appeared with some hot water.

I saw that M. Louis de Franchi had trained this valet really rather well.

Lucien had already asked twice over whether I was awake, and had declared that at half-past nine, if I still wasn't up and about, he would come into my room.

It was twenty-five past nine, so I did not have to wait for him to appear.

This time, he was dressed in French style, and elegant French style at that. He was wearing a black coat, an eye-catching waistcoat, and a pair of white trousers – for, in early March, people have already been wearing white trousers for some time in Corsica.

He saw that I was looking at him in some surprise.

'You seem to be admiring my clothes,' he said; 'it's further proof that I am becoming civilised.'

'Yes, my word it is,' I replied, 'and I have to tell you I'm really rather surprised to find such a fine tailor in Ajaccio. In my velvet jacket, I'm going to look like a perfect Parisian, compared to you.'

'But my outfit is pure Humann;[15] no more than that, my dear guest. As my brother and I are of exactly the same size, he played a trick on me – he sent me a complete wardrobe, and I wear it, as you can see, only on great occasions: when the Prefect passes by; when the General in command of the ninety-sixth *département* is doing his round of duty; or else when I receive a guest such as you, and this piece of good fortune is combined with an event as solemn as the one about to take place.'

There was in this young man a permanent sense of irony, the product of a superior mind. It made whoever he was talking to feel ill at ease, but it never went beyond perfect good manners.

So I contented myself with bowing in sign of thanks, as he put on, with all the usual precautions, a pair of yellow gloves that had been fitted to his hand by Boivin or Roussaux.

Dressed like this, he really did look like an elegant Parisian.

In the meantime, I too finished dressing.

The clock chimed a quarter to ten.

'Well now,' he said, 'if you wish to see the show, I think that it's time for us to take our seats in the stalls – unless, that is, you would prefer to have breakfast, which would be much more sensible, in my opinion.'

'Thank you; I rarely eat before eleven o'clock; so I can cope with the two activities at once.'

'Come along then.'

I picked up my hat and followed him.

11

From the top of the flight of eight steps giving access to the door of the castle where Mme de Franchi and her son lived, one looked out over the square.

This square now looked quite different from the day before: it was very crowded. But this throng of people was composed entirely of women and children under twelve: not a single man could be seen.

On the first step of the church stood a man solemnly swathed in a *tricolore* scarf: this was the Mayor.

On the porch, another man dressed in black was sitting at a table. Within reach lay a piece of paper covered in scrawled writing. This man was the notary: and the scrawled piece of paper was the act of reconciliation.

I took my seat on one side of the table with Orlandi's sponsors. On the other side were Colona's sponsors. Lucien took his place behind the notary, who represented both sides.

At the far end of the church, in the choir, you could see the priests all ready to say Mass.

The clock struck ten.

At that very moment, a shudder ran through the crowd, and everyone turned to look towards the two ends of the street, if one can call 'street' the irregular interval left by the caprice of some fifty or so houses built here and there just as their proprietors wished.

Immediately we saw, on the side nearest the mountain, Orlandi; and, on the side nearest the river, Colona. Each was followed by his supporters; but, as the programme that had been drawn up decreed, not one was carrying his weapons; had it not been for their somewhat rebarbative faces, they would have looked just like honest churchwardens following a procession.

The two heads of the two parties formed a decided contrast. Orlandi, as I said, was tall, slim, tanned, agile.

Colona was short, thickset, sturdy; his hair and beard were red, short and curly.

They were both bearing an olive branch, the symbolic emblem of the peace they were about to seal – a poetic invention of the Mayor's.

Colona was also holding by its legs a white hen, meant as a form of damages to replace the hen that, ten years earlier, had given birth to the quarrel.

The hen was alive.

This point had long been discussed and had almost brought the whole process to a halt, as Colona regarded it as a double humiliation to have to hand over a living hen when his aunt had flung a dead one at the face of Orlandi's cousin.

However, by dint of logic, Lucien had persuaded Colona to hand over the hen just as, by dint of dialectic, he had persuaded Orlandi to receive it.

Just as the two enemies appeared, the bells, which for a moment had fallen silent, started pealing out.

When they saw each other, Orlandi and Colona both gave a start, indicating their obvious mutual revulsion; however, they continued on their way.

Just opposite the church door, they halted some four paces away from each other.

If, three days earlier, these two men had met at a distance of a hundred paces, one would certainly have fallen where he stood.

For five minutes there was a silence, not only in the two groups, but also throughout the crowd. Despite the conciliatory purpose of the ceremony, there was nothing pacific about this silence.

Then the Mayor spoke.

'Well,' he said, 'Colona, don't you know that you should speak first?'

Colona pulled himself together and uttered a few words in Corsican patois.

I gathered that he was expressing his regret that he had been in a state of vendetta with his fine neighbour Orlandi over the past ten years, and that he was here to offer him, in reparation, the white hen he was holding.

Orlandi waited for his adversary's sentence to come to a definite end, and replied with a few other Corsican words that were a promise on his part to remember nothing but the solemn reconciliation that was taking place under the solemn auspices of the Mayor, with M. Lucien as arbitrator, and the notary to record the event.

Then the two of them again fell silent.

'Well, gentlemen,' said the Mayor, 'it had been agreed, if I remember rightly, that there would be a handshake.'

The two enemies instinctively put their hands behind their backs.

The Mayor came down off the step on which he was standing, took Colona's hand from behind his back, and then Orlandi's from behind his; and, after a few efforts that he attempted, smilingly, to conceal from his charges, he succeeded in joining the two hands.

The notary seized his moment; he stood up and read out – while the Mayor still held the two hands firmly together (they initially did all in their power to break loose, but finally resigned themselves to remaining clasped) – the following:

'WE, *Giuseppe-Antonio Sarrola, royal notary in Sullacaro, province of Sartène, attest that:*

'On the main square of the village, opposite the church, in the presence of the Mayor, the sponsors and the whole population;

'Between Gateano-Orso Orlandi, known as Orlandini;

'And Marco-Vincenzio Colona, known as Schioppone;

'It has been solemnly decreed THAT:

'From this day, 4th March 1841, henceforth, the vendetta declared ten years ago between them will cease.

'From the same day henceforth, they will live together as good neighbours and associates, as did their parents before the unfortunate affair which sowed disunion between their families and their friends.

'In pledge of which they have signed these presents, under the porch of the village church, with M. Polo Arbori, Mayor of the township, M. Lucien de Franchi, arbitrator, the sponsors of each of the two signatories, and us, the notary.

'Sullacaro, 4th March 1841.'

I was impressed to see that, in an excess of prudence, the notary had not uttered the slightest word about the hen that put Colona in such a difficult position vis-à-vis Orlandi.

Also, Colona's face lit up in direct proportion as Orlandi's darkened. The latter looked at the hen he was holding, and was clearly sorely tempted to fling it into Colona's face. But a glance from Lucien de Franchi nipped this wicked intention in the bud.

The Mayor saw there was no time to lose; he climbed backwards up the step, still holding the two hands together, without taking his eyes for a single moment off the newly reconciled men.

Then, so as to pre-empt the new argument that would not fail to arise at the moment of signing, given that each of the two adversaries would obviously regard it as a concession if he were first to sign, he took the quill and signed himself, and, transforming shame into honour, handed the quill to Orlandi, who took it from his hands, signed, and handed it to Lucien who, employing the same pacific subterfuge, handed it in turn to Colona, who made his cross.

At that very moment, the sound of singing echoed from the church, like a *Te Deum* after a victory.

Then we all signed, without distinction or rank or title, just as, a hundred and twenty-three years earlier, the nobles of France had signed the protest against the duc du Maine.[16]

Then the day's two heroes entered the church and went to kneel on either side of the choir, each in the place set apart for him.

I saw that from this moment onwards, Lucien's mind was perfectly easy: it was all over, the reconciliation was sworn, not only before men, but also before God.

The rest of the service proceeded without any noteworthy event.

Once Mass was over, Orlandi and Colona came out with the same ceremonial dignity.

At the door, on the Mayor's invitation, they again held out their hands to one another; then they each set off, with their respective trains of friends and relatives, to his house, where neither of them had been for three years.

As for Lucien and myself, we returned to the house of Mme de Franchi, where dinner was awaiting us.

It was easy for me to see, from the increased attention paid to me, that Lucien had read my name over my shoulder just as I was adding it to the bottom of the document, and that this name was not altogether unknown to him.

That morning, I had informed Lucien of my resolve to leave after dinner; I needed as a matter of urgency to return to Paris for the rehearsals of my play *A Marriage under Louis XV*, and, despite the insistent requests of both mother and son, I persisted in my first decision.

Lucien then asked me if he could take advantage of my offer and write to his brother, and Mme de Franchi, who, under her ancient strength, concealed a mother's heart, made me promise that I personally would deliver this letter to her son.

This would be of no great inconvenience for me: Louis de Franchi, being a true Parisian, lived at no. 7, rue du Helder.[17]

I asked to see Lucien's room one last time. He himself took me there and, pointing to everything in it, told me, 'You know that if anything here takes your fancy, you must take it: it's yours.'

I went over and took down a dagger placed in a rather dark corner which suggested that it was of no great value, and as I had seen Lucien glancing curiously at my hunting belt and praising it, asked him to accept it from me as a gift: he had the good taste to take it without obliging me to ask him twice.

Just then, Griffo appeared at the door.

He had come to inform me that the horse was saddled and that the guide was waiting for me.

I had with me the gift that I'd chosen for Griffo; it was a kind of hunting knife, with two pistols attached on either side of the blade and with batteries concealed in the handle.

I'd never seen anyone looking quite so delighted.

I went downstairs and found Mme de Franchi waiting for me; she wanted to wish me *bon voyage*, here at the foot of the stairs, the same place where she had bid me welcome. I kissed her hand; I felt the greatest respect for this woman, so simple and at the same time so dignified.

Lucien led me to the door.

'On any other day but this,' he said, 'I would saddle up my horse and go with you to the other side of the mountain; but today I dare not leave Sullacaro, in case one or other of our two new friends does something stupid.'

'And you're right to do so,' I told him; 'as for me, you can be sure that I'm really glad to have seen such a new ceremony in Corsica as the one I've just attended.'

'Yes indeed, you should be glad; you've seen something that must have made our ancestors spin in their graves.'

'That I can understand; in their day, a person's word was sacred enough for them not to have needed a notary in any process of reconciliation!'

'Our ancestors would never have been reconciled in the first place.'

He held his hand out to me.

'Aren't you going to ask me to embrace your brother on your behalf?' I asked him.

'Yes, of course, if it's not too much bother.'

'Well then, let's embrace each other; I can only give back what I have received.'

We embraced each other.

'Won't I see you again one day?' I asked him.

'Yes, if you come back to Corsica.'

'No, I mean if you come to Paris.'

'I'll never go,' replied Lucien.

'In any case, you'll find visiting cards with my name on your brother's mantelpiece. Don't forget the address.'

'I promise you that, if anything at all were to take me to the continent, you'd be the first person I'd visit.'

'Good then; that's settled.'

He held his hand out to me one last time, and we separated; but his eyes followed me all the way down the street leading to the river.

Things were pretty quiet in the village, although there was still that buzz that follows great events, and as I headed off I gazed at each door in turn, as if expecting to see Orlandi, my protégé, emerging. If truth be told, I deserved some thanks from him and had not received any.

But then I left behind the last house in the village, and advanced into the countryside without seeing anyone who resembled him.

I thought I must have been completely forgotten, and I have to say that, in the midst of the great preoccupations that must have been weighing on Orlandi on a day like this, I could easily forgive him for forgetting me, when, all of a sudden, on reaching the maquis of Bicchisano, I saw a man emerging from the thickets. He placed himself in the middle of the road, and I immediately recognised him as being the man whom, in all my French impatience, and being accustomed to Parisian politeness, I had been criticising for his ingratitude.

I noticed that he had already had time to put on the same clothes as when he appeared to me in the ruins of Vicentello – he was wearing his cartridge belt, from which there hung his inseparable pistol, and he was carrying his rifle.

When I was twenty paces from him, he took off his hat. I for my part spurred on my horse so as not to keep him waiting.

'Monsieur,' he said to me, 'I could not let you leave Sullacaro like this without thanking you for the honour you have shown a poor peasant like myself by acting as a witness;

and since at the time my heart was not at ease and my tongue was not free, I came to wait for you here.'

'Thank you,' I replied. 'But there was no need for you to go out of your way like this, and the honour was entirely mine.'

'Anyway,' continued the bandit, 'what do you expect, Monsieur? You can't lose the habits of four years in a single moment. The mountain air is terrible; once you've breathed it, you cannot breathe easily anywhere else. Just now, in those wretched houses, I kept thinking every minute that the roof was going to fall in on my head.'

'But,' I replied, 'you're still going to resume your usual lifestyle. You have a house, so I've heard, with a field and a vineyard?'

'Yes, of course; but my sister used to look after the house, and the people from Lucca were there to plough my field and harvest my grapes. We Corsicans don't work.'

'What do you do, then?'

'We inspect the workers, we stroll around with our rifles on our shoulders, we go hunting.'

'Well, my dear Monsieur Orlandi,' I said to him, holding out my hand, 'happy hunting! But remember that my honour, like yours, is pledged to ensuring that from now on you will only shoot at mouflons, deer, boar, pheasants and partridges, and never at Marco-Vicenzio Colona, nor at anyone from his family.'

'Ah, your Excellency,' replied my protégé with an expression on his face that I had never seen before, except on the faces of lawyers from Normandy, 'the hen he gave back to me was really skinny!'

And without adding another word, he flung off into the maquis where he disappeared.

I continued on my way, mulling over the probability that this would cause a new breach between Orlandis and Colonas.

That evening, I stayed over in Albiteccia. The next day, I arrived in Ajaccio.

A week later, I was in Paris.

12

The very same day I arrived, I presented myself at the home of M. Louis de Franchi; he had gone out.

I left my visiting card, with a note saying that I had just arrived straight from Sullacaro, and that I had a letter for him from M. Lucien, his brother. I asked him when he would be at home, adding that I had promised to hand this letter over to him in person. The servant led me to his master's study so that I could write these words there; my way to the study led me through both the dining room and the salon.

I looked all around with a curiosity that the reader will easily understand, and I recognised the same tastes that I had already glimpsed at Sullacaro; but these tastes were now heightened by Parisian elegance. M. Louis de Franchi seemed to have a charming bachelor apartment.

The following day, as I was getting dressed – it must have been at about eleven o'clock in the morning – my servant announced that M. de Franchi in turn had come to pay me a visit. I ordered that he be shown into the salon, offered the newspapers, and told that I would be his to command in a moment.

And so, five minutes later, I walked into the salon.

At the noise I made on entering, M. de Franchi, who – no doubt to be polite – had started to read one of my columns that, in those days, used to appear in *La Presse*, looked up.

I stopped, rooted to the spot at the way he so resembled his brother.

He rose to his feet.

'Monsieur,' he said, 'I could hardly believe my good fortune when, yesterday, I read the note that my servant handed to me when I got home. I made him describe you to me twenty times over, so as to assure myself that the description tallied with your portraits; finally, this morning, feeling impatient both to see you and to have news of my family, I presented myself at your home without paying much attention to what time it was; and I fear I may have come rather early in the day as a result.'

'Excuse me,' I replied, 'if I don't reply to your gracious compliment straight away; but I have to confess, Monsieur, that as I look at you, I ask myself whether it is Monsieur Louis or Monsieur Lucien de Franchi with whom I have the honour to speak.'

'Ah yes… We really do look alike, don't we?' he replied with a smile, 'and when I was still in Sullacaro, there was hardly anyone apart from my brother and myself who didn't occasionally get us mixed up. However, unless he has forsworn his Corsican habits since I left, you must have seen him constantly dressed in an outfit that makes it possible to tell the difference between us.'

'Indeed,' I replied, 'chance so decreed that, when I left him, he was, apart from his white trousers – which are not yet in season here in Paris – dressed exactly as you are: as a result, to distinguish between your presence and his memory, I do not even have that difference of costume to which you refer. But,' I continued, taking the letter from my wallet, 'I can well understand that you must be eager to have news of your family; so please take this letter, which I would have left at your home yesterday had I not promised Madame de Franchi to deliver it to you in person.'

'And when you left, everyone was in good health?'

'Yes, but they were worried.'

'About me?'

'About you. But please read the letter.'

'With your permission…?'

'But of course!'

M. de Franchi unsealed the letter, while I rolled a couple of cigarettes.

Meanwhile, my eyes followed him as he quickly read through his brother's epistle; from time to time, he smiled as he murmured:

'Ah, my dear Lucien! My kind mother!… Yes… yes… I see…'

I had still not got over that strange resemblance; and yet, as Lucien had told me I would, I could detect more pallor in his complexion and a clearer pronunciation of the French language.

'Well,' I resumed when he had finished, offering him a cigarette that he lit from mine, 'you will have seen, as I said, that your family was worried – and I am happy to see they were wrong to be so.'

'No,' he said sadly, 'not altogether wrong. I haven't been ill, admittedly; but I have fallen prey to a rather intense bout of melancholy which, I have to admit, was further increased by the idea that, by suffering here, I was making my brother suffer back home.'

'Monsieur Lucien had already told me what you have just told me, Monsieur; but to be perfectly honest, for me to believe that something so extraordinary was the truth and not some quirky idea of his, I needed the proof that I now have before my eyes; so, are you yourself convinced, Monsieur, that the malaise your brother experienced back home arose from the suffering that you were undergoing here?'

'Yes, Monsieur, absolutely.'

'Then,' I replied, 'as your affirmative reply has the result of making me doubly interested in whatever happens to you, allow me to ask you, out of sympathetic interest and not mere curiosity, whether the bout of melancholy you mentioned just now has passed, and whether you are on the road to recovery?'

'Ah, good Lord! As you know, Monsieur,' he replied, 'the most intense pains are dulled with time, and, so long as no accident poisons the wound in my heart, well, it will continue to bleed for a while, and then eventually scar over. In the meanwhile, please accept all my thanks again, and grant me permission to come and talk to you every so often about Sullacaro.'

'With the greatest pleasure,' I said; 'but why don't we continue the conversation right now? It is as pleasant for me as it is for you to talk of these things. Look, here's my servant, he's come to announce that breakfast is served. Do me the pleasure of having a cutlet with me, and then we can chat away to our hearts' content.'

'That's impossible, to my great regret. Yesterday I received a letter from the Minister of Justice, requesting me to present myself at his Ministry at midday today. You will easily understand that, as a poor little budding lawyer, I can't keep such an important personage waiting.'

'Oh... it's probably over the Orlandi and Colona affair that he's asked to see you.'

'I presume so, and as my brother tells me that the quarrel has been settled...'

'In the presence of a notary – of that I can assure you; I added my signature to the contract as the sponsor of Orlandi.'

'Yes, my brother mentioned that. – Listen,' he said to me, taking out his watch, 'it will very soon be midday; I must first go and tell the Justice Minister that my brother has fulfilled my pledge.'

'Oh, he did so with religious scruple, I can assure you.'

'That dear Lucien! I knew that, even though it wasn't really what he wanted, he would do so.'

'Yes, and he deserves some gratitude; I can tell you that the effort took its toll on him.'

'We can talk about all that a little later on; as you will understand, it is a great happiness for me to see my mother, my brother, and my native land again, as you summon them up to my mind's eye! So, if you don't mind telling me when you are at home…'

'It's rather difficult right now. Over the next few days, I'm going to be here, there and everywhere. But why don't you tell me where I can find you?'

'Listen,' he said, 'tomorrow is *mi-carême*,[18] isn't it?'

'Tomorrow?'

'Yes.'

'And?'

'Are you going to the Opera ball?'

'Yes and no. Yes, if you are asking me so that we can meet there; no, if there's no other reason for me to go.'

'Well, *I* have to go; I have no choice…'

'Aha!' I said with a smile, 'I can see that, as you were saying just now, time dulls the most intense pains, and the wound in your heart will scar over.'

'You're wrong. By going there, I will probably find new causes of pain.'

'Well, don't go!'

'Ah, good Lord – does anyone do what they want to do in this world? I'm being dragged there in spite of myself; I am going where Fate impels me. It would be better if I didn't go, that much I know – but I'm still going.'

'So, see you tomorrow, at the Opera?'

'Yes.'

'What time?'

'Half-past midnight, if you like.'

'And where?'

'In the foyer. Half an hour later I'm meeting somebody by the clock.'

'That sounds fine.'

We shook hands, and he hurried out.

It was almost midday.

As for me, I filled that afternoon and the whole of the following day with the errands that a man who has just been travelling for eighteen months cannot avoid.

And that night, at half-past midnight, I was at the place arranged.

Louis kept me waiting for a while; he had been following down the corridors a masked figure he'd thought he'd recognised; but the masked figure had vanished into the crowd, and he had not been able to catch up.

I wanted to talk about Corsica; but Louis was too preoccupied to follow such a serious topic of conversation; his eyes were constantly fixed on the clock, and all of a sudden he left me, exclaiming:

'Ah, here is my bouquet of violets!'

And he dived through the crowd to reach a woman who, indeed, was holding an enormous bouquet of violets.

As, luckily for the people strolling round, there were bouquets of every kind in the foyer, I myself was soon accosted by a bouquet of camellias – here to congratulate me on my safe return to Paris.

The bouquet of camellias was followed by a bouquet of roses decorated with pompons. And the bouquet of roses with pompons by a bouquet of heliotropes.

Finally, I was on my fifth bouquet when I bumped into D**.

'Ah, so it's you, my dear fellow!' he said. 'Welcome! You've come at just the right time; we're having supper this evening at my place, with…' and here he named three or four of the friends we had in common – 'and we're counting on you.'

'Thank you so much, my dear chap,' I replied, 'but although I would be extremely happy to accept your invitation, I can't: I'm here with someone.'

'But I thought it went without saying that everyone can bring his special somebody along; it's been agreed that there will be six carafes of water on the table, and their only purpose will be to keep the bouquets fresh.'

'Oh but, my dear friend, that's where you're wrong – I don't have any bouquets to put in your carafes: I'm with a friend.'

'Ah, but you know the proverb, "The friends of our friends…"'

'He's a young man that you don't know.'

'Well, you can introduce us.'

'I'll suggest that to him, I'm sure he'll be delighted.'

'Yes, and if he refuses, bring him along by force.'

'I'll do what I can, I promise you… At what time is supper being served?'

'Three o'clock; but as we'll be staying at table until six, you have a wide margin of time.'

'Good.'

A bouquet of forget-me-nots, who had perhaps heard the last part of our conversation, then took D**'s arm and led him away.

A few moments later, I came across Louis who, in all probability, had done with his bouquet of violets. Since the conversation of my domino-wearing companion was far from brilliant, I sent him to go and converse with one of my friends, and I took Louis by the arm.

'Well,' I said to him, 'did you learn what you wanted to know?'

'Oh, good Lord, yes: as you know, in general, at a masked ball we are only ever told things that ought to be kept from us.'

'My poor friend,' I told him. 'Forgive me for calling you that, but it seems to me that I've known you ever since I've known your brother… Let's see… You're unhappy, aren't you?… So what's wrong?'

'Oh, good Lord, nothing worth talking about.'

I saw that he wanted to keep his secret, and fell silent.

We walked around for a while in silence; I paid little attention to the people around me, but his eyes were for ever on the alert, examining every domino who came within sight.

'Look,' I told him, 'do you know what you ought to do?'

He started, like a man whose train of thought has suddenly been disturbed.

'Me?… No!… What did you say? Sorry…'

'I have a suggestion to make – something you might enjoy, and that you seem in need of.'

'Namely?'

'Come and have supper at a friend's house with me.'

'Oh no, absolutely not… I'd be a very glum guest.'

'Pah! People will be talking any old nonsense, and that will cheer you up.'

'Anyway, I'm not invited.'

'There you're wrong: you *are* invited.'

'It's very kind of your gentle host, but, my word, I don't feel worthy…'

At that moment we came across D**. He seemed very busy with his bouquet of forget-me-nots.

But he still saw me.

'Well then,' he said, 'it's settled then? Three o'clock.'

'It's not settled at all, my dear chap; I won't be able to join you.'

'Well, you can go to the devil, then!'

And he continued on his way.

'Who is that fellow?' Louis asked me, obviously just for the sake of asking.

'Oh, that's D**, one of our friends, a very witty chap, despite running one of our foremost papers.'

'Monsieur D**!' exclaimed Louis, 'Monsieur D**! Do you know him?'

'Of course; we've known each other as business partners and indeed friends for two or three years.'

'So is he the one who's invited you to have supper with him later on tonight?'

'Exactly.'

'And you were offering to take me to his place?'

'Yes.'

'That's completely different, then – I accept, and with the greatest pleasure!'

'Excellent! You took some persuading!'

'Perhaps I shouldn't go,' Louis continued, with a sad smile; 'but you know what I was telling you yesterday: we don't go where we would like to go, we go where Fate impels us; and the proof is the fact that I would have done better not to come here this evening.'

Just then, we again crossed D**.

'My dear chap,' I said, 'I've changed my mind.'

'So you *will* be joining us?'

'Yes.'

'Ah, bravo! But there's one thing I need to tell you.'

'What's that?'

'Whoever has supper with us this evening must also have supper with us the day after tomorrow.'

'In virtue of what law?'

'In virtue of a wager laid with Château-Renaud.'

Louis's arm was hanging on mine, and I felt him give a start.

I turned to look at him; but although he was paler than he had been a moment before, his face had remained impassive.

'And what is this wager?' I asked D**.

'Oh, it would take too long to tell you here. Then there is someone else involved in this wager, and if that person heard of the wager, it might lead to its being lost.'

'Excellent! See you at three.'

'See you at three.'

We again went our separate ways. As I passed in front of the clock, I glanced at the time: it was two thirty-five.

'Do you know this Monsieur de Château-Renaud?' Louis asked me, trying in vain to conceal the eagerness in his voice.

'Only by sight; I've sometimes seen him at social gatherings.'

'So he's not one of your friends?'

'He's not even an acquaintance.'

'Ah! That's good!' said Louis.

'Why?'

'No reason.'

'But do *you* know him?'

'Indirectly.'

In spite of this evasive reply, it was easy for me to see that, between M. de Franchi and M. de Château-Renaud, there existed one of those mysterious relationships of which a woman provides the guiding thread. My intuition then told me that it would be better for my companion if we both returned to our respective homes.

'Look here,' I said, 'Monsieur de Franchi, will you take a piece of advice from me?'

'What do you mean?'

'Let's not go to supper at D**'s.'

'Why ever not? Won't he be expecting us, or rather, hadn't you told him you were bringing a guest?'

'Indeed; but that's not the reason.'

'Why, then?'

'Because I just think it would be better for us not to go.'

'But look, you must have some reason for changing your mind; just now you were insisting on taking me, even though I was pretty reluctant.'

'We'd only be going to meet Monsieur de Château-Renaud.'

'All the better! He's said to be a very pleasant fellow, and I'd be delighted to get to know him better.'

'Oh, all right then,' I replied. 'Let's go, since that's what you want.'

We went down to collect our jackets.

D** lived very close to the Opera. It was a warm night: I reflected that the fresh air would always calm my companion down a little. I suggested we walk there, and he agreed.

13

In the salon we met several of my friends, habitués of the Opera foyer, denizens of the most elegant box seats, de B**, L**, V**, and A**. Furthermore, as I had suspected, two or three dominos had removed their masks and were holding their bouquets as they waited for the moment to put them into carafes of water.

I introduced Louis de Franchi to several of the people there; I don't need to say that he was made to feel most welcome by each and every one of them.

Ten minutes later, D** in turn came in, bringing with him the bouquet of forget-me-nots, who removed her mask with a sense of relief and an eagerness that showed her to be both a pretty woman, and also a woman used to this kind of party.

I introduced M. de Franchi to D**.

'Now,' said de B**, 'if everyone has been introduced, could we all take our places at table?'

'Everyone has been introduced, but not all the guests have arrived,' replied D**.

'So who are we still waiting for?'

'We're still waiting for Château-Renaud.'

'Ah, that's true. Isn't there some wager…?' asked V**.

'Yes, a wager that he will buy supper for twelve people if he doesn't bring along a certain lady who he has promised will come with him.'

'So who is this lady?' asked the bouquet of forget-me-nots. 'She must be rather a wild woman if people are laying such wagers on her!'

I looked at de Franchi; he seemed outwardly calm, but he was as pale as death.

'My word,' replied D**, 'I don't think there's any great indiscretion in giving you the name of the masked figure, especially as, in all probability, you won't know her. It's Madame…'

Louis placed his hand on D**'s arm.

'Monsieur,' he said, 'as we have become acquainted only recently, please grant me a favour.'

'What favour, Monsieur?'

'Don't give the name of the person who is supposed to be coming with Monsieur de Château-Renaud: you know that she is a married woman.'

'Yes, but her husband is in Smyrna, or India, or Mexico, I don't know where. When you have a husband so far away, you know, it's as if you didn't have one at all.'

'Her husband is returning in a few days; I know him – he's a real gentleman, and, if possible, I would like to spare him the sorrow of learning, on his return, that his wife has done such a foolish thing.'

'In that case, please excuse me,' said D**, 'I was unaware that you knew the lady; I was even unsure whether she was married; but since you are acquainted with her, and since you also know her husband…'

'I do know them.'

'We will be the soul of discretion in the matter. Ladies and gentlemen, whether Château-Renaud comes or does not come, whether he comes alone or accompanied by someone else, whether he wins or loses his wager, I would ask you to keep this whole business secret.'

Everyone unanimously promised to keep the secret, probably not out of any deep-seated sense of social niceties, but because they were all hungry and consequently in a hurry to sit down at table.

'Thank you, Monsieur,' said de Franchi to D**, holding his hand out to him; 'I can assure you that you have just acted like a thorough gentleman.'

We moved to the dining room, and everyone took their places. Two were still vacant: those of Château-Renaud and the person he was supposed to be bringing.

The servant came over to remove the places set for them.

'No,' said the master of the house, 'leave them there; Château-Renaud has until four o'clock. At four, you can clear away their places; on the stroke of four, he will have lost.'

I could not take my eyes off M. de Franchi. I saw him turn his eyes to the clock: the time was three forty.

'Are you feeling all right?' asked Louis coldly.

'It's nothing to do with me,' said D**, with a laugh; 'it's to do with Château-Renaud. I have set my clock by his watch so that he can't complain that he was cheated.'

'Now then, gentlemen!' said the bouquet of forget-me-nots, 'for God's sake! Since we can't talk about Château-Renaud and his unknown lady, let's not talk about them; otherwise we'll fall into symbols, allegories and enigmas, and that's deadly boring.'

'You're right, Est**,' replied V**; 'there are so many women one cannot talk about and who want nothing more than to be talked about.'

'Let's drink to the health of those ladies,' said D**.

And they started to fill our glasses with iced champagne. Each guest had his own bottle.

I noticed that Louis barely grazed his glass with his lips.

'Go on, drink,' I told him. 'You can see he's not going to come.'

'It's still only a quarter to four,' he said. 'At four o'clock, however far behind I've been left, I promise you I'll catch up with whoever's been drinking the deepest.'

'That's the spirit!'

As we exchanged these words in low tones, the conversation was spreading and becoming noisier. Every so often, D** and Louis glanced at the hands of the clock, which continued to advance in their impassive way, in spite of the impatience of the two people who kept staring at it.

At five to four, I looked at Louis.

'Your health!' I told him.

He took up his glass with a smile and raised it to his lips.

He had drunk about half of it when the doorbell chimed.

I would never have believed that he could grow any paler, but I was wrong.

'It's him,' I said.

'Yes, but maybe she's not with him,' he replied.

'That's what we're just about to see.'

The doorbell had attracted everyone's attention, and the deepest silence had immediately followed the hubbub of conversation all around – and sometimes across – the table.

We then heard what sounded like an argument in the antechamber.

D** immediately rose and went to open the door.

'I recognised her voice,' Louis told me, seizing me by the wrist and gripping it tightly.

'Come now, show some courage, be a man,' I replied. 'It's clear that, if she is coming to have supper at the home of a man she does not know, and with other people she does not know either, she must be a tart, and a tart isn't worth the love of a gentleman.'

'But please, Madame,' D** was saying in the antechamber, 'do go in; I assure you that we are all friends here.'

'But do go in, my dear Emilie,' M. de Château-Renaud was saying; 'you don't have to take your mask off if you'd rather not.'

'The wretch!' murmured Louis de Franchi.

Just then, a woman entered, dragged rather than led in by D**, who thought he was fulfilling his duty as master of the house, and by Château-Renaud.

'Three minutes to four,' Château-Renaud murmured to D**.

'Very well, dear chap, you have won…'

'Not yet, Monsieur,' said the unknown young woman, addressing Château-Renaud, and drawing herself up to her full height; 'now I understand why you were so insistent… You had laid a wager to bring me here – is that it?'

Château-Renaud was silent. She turned to address D**.

'Since this man won't answer, *you*, Monsieur, answer instead,' she said: 'it's true, isn't it, that Monsieur de Château-Renaud had laid a wager that he'd bring me to supper at your home?'

'I cannot hide from you, Madame, the fact that Monsieur de Château-Renaud had flattered me with that hope.'

'Well, Monsieur de Château-Renaud has lost. I didn't know where he was taking me, and I thought I was going to have supper at the home of one of my lady friends; and since I did not come here of my own free will, Monsieur de Château-Renaud must, it seems to me, forfeit his winnings.'

'But now that you *are* here, my dear Emilie,' said M. de Château-Renaud, 'you will stay, won't you? Look, we have a goodly company of menfolk and a merry company of womenfolk.'

'Now that I *am* here,' said the unknown woman, 'I will thank Monsieur, who is apparently the master of the house, for the kind welcome he has given me; but as, unfortunately, I cannot accept his gracious invitation, I will ask Monsieur Louis de Franchi to give me his arm and take me back to my home.'

Louis de Franchi leapt forward. In a trice he was standing between M. de Château-Renaud and the unknown woman.

84

'I would have you observe, Madame,' said Château-Renaud, between clenched teeth, 'that it was I who brought you here and that, in consequence, it is for me to take you home.'

'Gentlemen,' said the unknown woman, 'there are five of you here, all men; I place myself under the safeguard of your honour; you will, I hope, prevent Monsieur de Château-Renaud from doing me violence.'

Château-Renaud made a movement; we all rose to our feet.

'Very well, Madame,' he said, 'you are free; I know with whom I now have to deal.'

'If it is myself, Monsieur,' said Louis de Franchi, with an hauteur impossible to describe, 'you will find me all day at home tomorrow: no. 7, rue du Helder.'

'Very well, Monsieur, perhaps I will be unable to present myself at your address in person; but I hope that in my stead, you will be happy to receive two of my friends.'

'I suppose I can't be surprised at you, Monsieur,' said Louis de Franchi, with a shrug, 'making such an arrangement in the presence of a lady. Come, Madame,' he continued, taking the arm of the unknown woman, 'you can rest assured that I thank you from the depths of my heart for the honour you do me.'

And the two of them left amid a deep silence.

'Well, gentlemen, what of it?' said Château-Renaud, when the door had closed behind them; 'I've lost, that's all. I will see you the evening after tomorrow, so long as we are all still here, at the *Frères-Provençaux*.'[19]

And he sat at one of the two empty places, and held out his glass to D**, who filled it to the brim.

However, as the reader will easily understand, in spite of the noisy hilarity of M. de Château-Renaud, the rest of the supper was a somewhat glum affair.

14

The next day – or rather, the very same day – I was at the door of M. Louis de Franchi at ten o'clock in the morning.

As I was climbing the stairs, I met two young men coming down: the one was evidently a man of the world; the other, decorated with the Legion of Honour, appeared (although in civilian costume) to be a soldier. I guessed that these two gentlemen were coming from M. Louis de Franchi's, and I gazed after them until they reached the foot of the stairs; then I carried on my way and rang the doorbell.

The servant came and opened the door; his master was in his study.

When he entered to announce me, Louis, who was sitting down and busy writing, looked round.

'Ah, just the man!' he said, crumpling up the note he had just started writing and throwing it on the fire, 'this note was for you, and I was about to send it to your address. That will be all, Joseph, please tell anyone else that I am not at home.'

The servant went out.

'Didn't you meet two gentlemen on the stairs?' continued Louis, pushing an armchair forward.

'Yes, and one of them was wearing a decoration.'

'The very same.'

'I guessed they had just come from seeing you.'

'You guessed correctly.'

'Had they come from Monsieur de Château-Renaud?'

'They're his seconds.'

'Damn! He seems to have taken the business seriously.'

'He could hardly have done otherwise, as I am sure you would agree,' replied Louis de Franchi.

'And they had come…?'

'To request me to send two of my friends to talk business with them. At that point I thought of you.'

'I am deeply honoured that you remembered me, but I cannot present myself at their address all by myself.'

'I have asked one of my friends, Baron Giordano Martelli, to come and have breakfast with me. At eleven o'clock he will be here. We'll have breakfast together, and, at midday, if you'll be so kind as to go and fetch these gentlemen – they have promised to be at home until three o'clock. Here are their names and addresses.'

Louis gave me their visiting cards.

The name of the one was Baron René de Châteaugrand, and the other was M. Adrien de Boissy.

The address of the first was no. 12, rue de la Paix.

The second, who – as I had guessed – was in the Army, was a lieutenant in our light cavalry in Africa, and his address was no. 29, rue de Lille.

I turned the visiting cards over several times in my hands.

'Well, what's the problem?' asked Louis.

'I'd like to know in all honesty whether you regard this business as serious. As you will understand, our whole conduct will depend on your opinion.'

'What do you mean? It's entirely serious! In any case, as you must have heard, I've placed myself at the disposal of Monsieur de Château-Renaud, and it is he who has sent me his seconds. I simply need to follow the procedure.'

'Yes, of course… but after all…'

'Out with it!' said Louis, with a smile.

'But, you know… one ought to know what you're fighting about. We can't see two men killing each other without at least knowing the reason why they are at daggers drawn. As you know, the position of a second is more serious than that of a duellist.'

'In that case I'll tell you briefly what lies behind this quarrel. Listen:

'When I arrived in Paris, one of my friends, captain of a frigate, introduced me to his wife. She was a beautiful woman, and she was young; seeing her made such a deep impression on me that I thought I might fall in love with her. So I took as little advantage as possible of the permission that had been granted me to visit them at home at any time of the day.

'My friend complained of my indifference, and so in all frankness I told him the truth. His wife was altogether too charming for me to run the risk of seeing her often. He smiled, gave me his hand, and insisted that I have dinner with him that very same day.

' "My dear Louis," he told me over dessert, "in three weeks' time I'm leaving for Mexico; I may be away for three months, for six months, perhaps even longer. We sailors sometimes know the hour of our departure, but never that of our return. I'm entrusting Emilie to you in my absence. Emilie, please treat Louis de Franchi as your brother."

'In reply, the young woman gave me her hand.

'I was stupefied: I could not think what to say, and I must have appeared a complete idiot to my future sister.

'And three weeks later, my friend did indeed depart.

'Throughout those three weeks, he had insisted that I go and dine with him and his family at least once a week.

'Emilie stayed with her mother: I don't need to tell you that her husband's trust had made her sacred to me. While I loved her more than a brother should, I only ever considered her as a sister.

'Six months went by.

88

'Emilie continued to live with her mother; when he left, her husband had insisted that she continue to receive guests. There was nothing my poor friend feared more than gaining a reputation for being a jealous man: the fact is, he adored Emilie, and he trusted her entirely.

'So Emilie continued to receive guests. In any case, her receptions were intimate affairs, and her mother's presence made it impossible for even the most malicious minds to find cause for criticism. So nobody dared to say a word that might cast a shadow over her reputation.

'Three months or so ago, Monsieur de Château-Renaud had himself announced.

'You believe in presentiments, don't you? When I saw him, I shuddered; he did not speak to me; he behaved the way a man of the world is expected to behave in a salon, and yet, when he went out, I hated him already.

'Why? I myself had no idea.

'Or rather, I had noticed that my feelings on seeing Emilie for the first time were the same feelings that he himself had experienced.

'It struck me that Emilie, for her part, had received him with an unaccustomed display of coquetry. I was probably wrong, but, as I have said, in the depths of my heart, I had not stopped loving Emilie, and I was jealous.

'And so, at her next evening reception, I did not let Monsieur de Château-Renaud out of my sight: perhaps he noticed the way I so insistently kept my eyes on him, and it seemed to me that, speaking to Emilie in a half-murmur, he was trying to make me look ridiculous.

'If I had merely listened to what my heart was telling me, I would have picked a quarrel with him that very evening, on some pretext or other, and fought a duel with him; but I kept my thoughts to myself, and told myself repeatedly that such behaviour would be absurd.

'Well, you will hardly be surprised to learn that every Friday became a day of torment for me.

'Monsieur de Château-Renaud is a real lion of the social world, a man of elegance and charisma. I recognised that, in many ways, he was my superior, but it seemed to me that Emilie placed him on a higher pedestal than he deserved.

'I soon noticed that I was not the only person to have noted Emilie's preference for Monsieur de Château-Renaud, and this preference increased in such a way, and eventually became so obvious, that one day, Giordano, who (like myself) was a frequent visitor to her home, mentioned it to me.

'From that time on my mind was made up; I resolved to speak of the matter to Emilie, convinced as I still was that she was simply being thoughtless, and that I needed only to open her eyes to her own behaviour – then she would stop indulging in what might have been thought of as open flirtation. But, to my great astonishment, Emilie refused to take my observations the least bit seriously; she merely told me I was crazy, and that anyone who shared my ideas was as crazy as I was.

'I persisted.

'Emilie replied that she would pay no attention to my views on such a matter, and that a man in love was bound to be prejudiced.

'I was thunderstruck; her husband had told her everything.

'From then on, as you will understand, my role – envisaged as that of a spurned and jealous lover – was bound to appear ridiculous and almost hateful; I stopped going to Emilie's home.

'Although I had ceased to attend her evening gatherings, I still heard about her; I still knew what she was doing, and it still made me very unhappy; people were starting to notice how Monsieur de Château-Renaud was courting her, and to talk openly about it.

'I resolved to write to her. I did so as gently as I could, begging her, in the name of her compromised honour, in the name of her absent husband who trusted her completely, to control herself. She did not reply.

'What do you expect? Love is independent of our will; the poor woman was in love, and, being in love, she was blind, or absolutely wished to be so.

'Some time later, I heard it being said quite openly that Emilie was the mistress of Monsieur de Château-Renaud.

'There are no words to express my suffering.

'It was then that my brother felt the effects of my own grief.

'Nearly a fortnight went by, and then you arrived.

'On the very same day when you presented yourself at my home, I had received an anonymous letter. This letter had come from an unknown lady who wished to meet me at the Opera ball.

'This lady told me that she had certain information to communicate to me about one of my lady friends; for the time being she contented herself with giving me the latter's first name.

'That name was "Emilie".

'I would recognise her from her bouquet of violets.

'That's why I'm telling you that I shouldn't have gone to that ball; but, let me say again, I was impelled by Fate.

'I went along; I found my domino waiting for me at the time and place indicated. The domino confirmed what I had already been told: Monsieur de Château-Renaud was Emilie's lover and, as I had guessed, or rather as I pretended to have guessed, the proof was that Monsieur de

Château-Renaud had laid a wager that he would be bringing his new mistress to supper at the home of Monsieur D**.

'As chance would have it, you know Monsieur D**; you had been invited to this supper; you were able to take a friend; you suggested taking me, and I accepted.

'The rest you know.

'Now, what can I do other than wait and accept whatever proposals are made to me?'

There was no answer to that: I merely bowed.

'But,' I resumed after a moment, feeling distinctly uneasy, 'I seem to remember – and I hope that I am mistaken – that your brother told me you have never touched pistol or sword.'

'That is true.'

'But in that case you are at the mercy of your opponent.'

'That's just too bad. God will provide!'

15

Just then, the valet announced Baron Giordano Martelli.

He, like Louis de Franchi, was a young Corsican from the province of Sartène; he was serving in the 11th regiment, where two or three admirable feats of arms had led to his appointment, at the age of twenty-three, to the rank of captain. It goes without saying that he was dressed in civilian clothes.

'Well,' he said, after greeting me, 'the business has finally reached the point it was bound to reach and, from what you wrote to me, you will in all probability be receiving a visit from the seconds of Monsieur de Château-Renaud later today.'

'They have been,' said Louis.

'Did they leave their names and addresses?'

'Here are their visiting cards.'

'Good! Your valet told me that our breakfast was ready; let's eat, and then we can go and pay them a visit.'

We moved to the dining room, and no further mention was made of the matter that had brought us together.

Only then did Louis question me about my journey to Corsica. I thus had a chance at last to tell him the full story with which the reader is already acquainted.

Now that the young man's mind was calmed by the idea that he would be fighting a duel the next day with M. de Château-Renaud, all his feelings for his native land and his family flooded back into his heart.

He made me repeat to him twenty times over what his brother and his mother had said. He was especially touched, knowing as he did the truly Corsican manners and customs of Lucien, to hear of the way he had taken the trouble to appease the quarrel between the Orlandis and the Colonas.

The clock chimed midday.

'I think – without in any way wishing to drive you away, Messieurs – that maybe it is time to return the visit of those gentlemen,' said Louis. 'If we leave it any longer, they might start to think we were being neglectful.'

'Oh, on that point, you can rest assured,' I rejoined; 'they left here barely two hours ago, and you needed time to get here.'

'That may be true,' said Baron Giordano, 'but Louis is right.'

'And now,' I said to Louis, 'we still need to know which weapon you prefer: sword or pistol.'

'Good Lord, as I've already told you, I really don't mind in the least, since I'm familiar with neither of them. In any case, Monsieur de Château-Renaud will spare me the difficulty of having to choose. He will no doubt regard himself as the injured party, and, as such, he will be able to choose whichever weapon he wants.'

'But it's not that clear on whose side the injury lies. You did nothing but give your arm to someone who was requesting it.'

'Listen,' said Louis, 'any discussion, in my opinion, might start to look like a desire to come to terms. My tastes are those of a man of peace, as you know; I am far from being a duellist, since this is the first duel I have ever fought; but it's exactly for all these reasons that I want to play the game well.'

'It's easy enough for you to say that, my dear fellow; you are merely playing with your life – and you're leaving the responsibility for what happens to *us*: we will have to explain things to your family.'

'Oh, you don't need to worry about any of that. I know my mother and my brother. They'll ask you: "Did Louis behave like a gentleman?", and when you reply, "Yes", they'll say, "That's good."'

'But, devil take it!… We still need to know which weapon you prefer.'

'Well, if they suggest the pistol, accept straight away.'

'That was just what I was thinking,' said the Baron.

'Very well, the pistol it is,' I replied, 'since that's what you have both decided. But the pistol is a nasty weapon.'

'Do I have time to learn how to handle a sword between now and tomorrow?'

'No. And yet, if Grisier[20] gives you a lesson, you might manage to defend yourself.'

Louis smiled.

'Believe me,' he said, 'whatever happens to me tomorrow is already written in the stars, and you and I can do whatever we want – it won't change a thing.'

Whereupon we shook his hand and went downstairs.

Our first visit was naturally to the home of our adversary's second who lived closest.

So we made our way to no. 12, rue de la Paix, where – as we have said – lived M. René de Châteaugrand.

The door was closed to everyone except those representing M. Louis de Franchi.

We told the valet of our mission, presented our visiting cards, and were immediately allowed in.

We found M. de Châteaugrand to be a most elegant man of the world. He refused to let us pay a visit to M. de Boissy; we need not trouble ourselves to do so, he told us – the two of them had agreed together that the first man to whom we presented ourselves would send for the other.

So he immediately sent his lackey to inform M. Adrien de Boissy that we were waiting for him.

As we waited, the matter that had brought us here was not mentioned once. We chatted about the races, hunting, and the opera.

M. de Boissy arrived after ten minutes.

These gentlemen did not even bring up the question of the choice of weapons: M. de Château-Renaud was equally familiar with both sword and pistol, and they were happy to let M. de Franchi – or chance – decide. They tossed a *louis d'or* in the air: heads for swords, tails for pistols. It was tails.

So it was decided that the duel would take place the following morning at nine o'clock, in the Bois de Vincennes; the adversaries would be placed at twenty paces from one another; someone would clap his hands three times, and on the third clap, they would fire.

We went to give this reply to M. de Franchi.

That same evening, I found, when I returned home, the visiting cards of MM. de Châteaugrand and de Boissy.

16

I had presented myself at the home of M. de Franchi at eight o'clock that evening, asking whether there was anything he would like me to do for him; but he had asked me to wait until the next day, replying, with a strange expression on his face, 'We need to sleep on it.'

And so, the next morning, instead of going to pick him up at eight o'clock, which would have given us plenty of time to get to the meeting place by nine, I was at Louis de Franchi's home at half-past seven.

He was already in his study, writing.

Hearing me open the door, he turned round.

He was very pale.

'Excuse me,' he said, 'I've just finished writing to my mother. Sit down, take a newspaper, if they've arrived; look, *La Presse*, for example, there's a wonderful column by Monsieur Méry.'[21]

I picked up the paper he had pointed to and sat down, astonished to see the contrast between the almost livid pallor of the young man's face and his gentle, grave, calm voice.

I tried to read, but I followed the lines of print mechanically with my eyes, and they made little real sense to my mind.

After five minutes, he said, 'I'm ready.'

He immediately rang for his valet.

'Joseph, tell visitors that I am not at home, not even for Giordano; take him into the salon; I wish to be alone with this gentleman for ten minutes, and nobody is to disturb us.'

The valet closed the door behind him.

'Well then,' he said, 'my dear Alexandre, Giordano is a Corsican, he has Corsican ideas, so I cannot trust him to do as I wish him to; I will simply ask him to keep my secret, that's all. As for you, you must promise to carry out my instructions to the letter.'

'Certainly! Isn't that the duty of a second?'

'A duty that is all the more real in that you may thus spare our family another misfortune.'

'Another misfortune?' I asked in astonishment.

'Look,' he said, 'this is what I have written to my mother; read this letter.'

I took the letter out of de Franchi's hands, and read with increasing astonishment.

My dear Mother,

If I didn't know that you were as strong as a Spartan and as submissive as a Christian, I would use every means possible to prepare you for the terrible event that is about to befall you; when you receive this letter, you will have only one son left.

Lucien, my excellent brother: you must love our mother on behalf of both of us!

The day before yesterday, I suffered a cerebral fever, but I paid little attention to the first symptoms; the doctor arrived too late! My dear mother, there is now no hope for me, unless a miracle happens – and what right do I have to hope that God will perform this miracle for me?

I am writing to you in a moment of lucidity; if I die, this letter will be posted a quarter of an hour after my death; for, in the selfishness of my love for you, I wish you to know that, at the moment of death, my only regret was that I would miss your tender love and that of my brother.

Farewell, my mother.

Do not weep; it was the soul that loved you and not the body, and, wherever it goes, the soul will continue to love you.

Farewell, Lucien.

Do not ever leave our mother, and remember that she has only you.

Your son,

Your brother,

– Louis de Franchi

After reading these last words, I turned to the man who had written them.

'Well,' I said to him, 'what is the meaning of all this?'

'Don't you understand?' he said to me.

'No.'

'I am going to be killed at ten minutes past nine.'

'You are going to be killed?'

'Yes.'

'But you are crazy! Why burden yourself with such an idea?'

'I am neither crazy nor is my mind burdened, my dear friend… I am forewarned, that is all.'

'Forewarned? And by whom?'

'Didn't my brother tell you,' Louis asked with a smile, 'that the males in our family enjoy a singular privilege?'

'True,' I replied, with an involuntary shudder; 'he mentioned apparitions.'

'That's it. Well, my father appeared to me last night; that's why you found me looking so pale; the sight of the dead does make the living turn pale.'

I gazed at him in amazement bordering on terror.

'You saw your father last night, you say?'

'Yes.'

'And he spoke to you?'

'He announced my death.'

'It was some terrible dream,' I said.

'It was a terrible reality.'

'Were you asleep?'

'I was awake… So don't you believe that a father can visit his son?'

I looked down; in my heart of hearts, I myself believed this was possible.

'How did it happen?' I asked.

'Oh, good Lord, the simplest, most natural way imaginable. I was reading as I waited for my father – I knew that, if I was running any risk, my father would appear to me. At midnight, the light of my lamp faded spontaneously, the door slowly swung open, and my father appeared.'

'But how?' I asked.

'But… just as when he was alive: wearing the clothes he usually wore – but he was very pale, and his eyes were expressionless.'

'Oh my God!…'

'Then he slowly approached my bed. I raised myself on one elbow.

'"Welcome, Father," I said to him.

'He approached me, and stared at me fixedly – and it was as if that dulled eye were animated by the strength of his fatherly feelings.'

'Go on… it's terrible!…'

'Then his lips started to move and, strange to relate, although his words did not produce any sound, I could hear them within myself, as distinct and vibrant as an echo.'

'And what did he say to you?'

'He said to me, "Remember God, my son!"

'"So, am I going to be killed in this duel?" I asked.

'I saw two tears drop from those expressionless eyes onto the spectre's pale face.

' "At what time?"

'He pointed to the clock. I followed his finger. It was ten past nine by the clock.

' "That is fine, Father," I then replied. "God's will be done. I am leaving my mother, true – but I will be coming to join you."

'Then a pale smile flitted across his lips, and, bidding me farewell with a wave of his hand, he turned away.

'The door opened spontaneously before him... He vanished, and the door closed behind him.'

This narrative was so simply and naturally told that it was clear that the scene which de Franchi was describing had really taken place, or that he had, as a result of an overburdened mind, been the plaything of an illusion that he had taken for reality, an illusion that was thus as terrible as the reality itself.

I wiped away the beads of sweat pouring from my forehead.

'Now,' continued Louis, 'you know my brother, don't you?'

'Yes.'

'What do you think he'll do if he learns that I have been killed in a duel?'

'He will leave Sullacaro that very same instant to come and fight a duel with the man who kills you.'

'Precisely, and, if he is killed in turn, my mother will be a widow three times over – widowed of her husband, and widowed of her two sons.'

'Ah, I see! That's dreadful!'

'And that's just what we need to prevent. That's why I decided to write this letter. If she thinks that I have died of a cerebral fever, my brother won't blame anybody, and my mother will be more easily consoled (thinking it is God's will that I have succumbed to an illness) than if she knows that I have been struck down by the hand of men. Unless...'

'Unless what…?' I repeated.

'Ah, no,' said Louis, 'I hope that doesn't happen.'

I saw that he was in the grip of a personal fear, and I didn't persist.

Just then, the door half opened.

'My dear de Franchi,' said the Baron de Giordano, 'I respected your instructions for as long as I could; but it is eight o'clock; we are supposed to be meeting at nine; we have a league and a half to travel, we need to be on our way.'

'I'm ready, my dear friend,' said Louis. 'Do come in. I have told this gentleman what I needed to tell him.'

He placed a finger to his lips as he gazed at me.

'As for you, my friend,' he continued, turning to the table and picking up a sealed letter; 'this is for you. If anything should happen to me, read this letter, and carry out, I beg you, my instructions.'

'Of course!'

'You've sorted out the weapons?'

'Yes,' I replied. 'But just as I was leaving, I noticed that one of the hammers was getting stuck. We'll pick up a box of pistols from Devisme[22] on our way.'

Louis smiled at me and offered me his hand. He had realised that I didn't want him to be killed with my pistols.

'Do you have a carriage?' asked Louis, 'or should Joseph go and get one?'

'I have my coupé,' said the Baron, 'and if we squeeze in, it will take all three of us. In any case, as we're a little late, we'll go faster with my horses than with the horses of a fiacre.'

'Let's go,' said Louis.

We went down. At the door, Joseph was waiting for us.

'Shall I go with Monsieur?' he asked.

'No, Joseph,' replied Louis, 'no, there's no need, I won't be requiring you.'

Then, hanging back a little, he said, pressing a small rouleau of gold into his hand, 'Here, my friend, this is for you: if, in my moments of bad temper, I have offended you, please forgive me.'

'Oh, Monsieur!' said Joseph, with tears in his eyes, 'what is the meaning of this?'

'Hush!' said Louis.

And, leaping into the carriage, he took his place between us.

'He was a good servant,' he said, glancing one last time at Joseph. 'If one or other of you could be of any assistance to him, I would be most grateful.'

'Are you dismissing him?' asked the Baron.

'No,' smiled Louis, 'I'm leaving him, that's all.'

We stopped at the door of Devisme's shop, just long enough to pick up a box of pistols, gunpowder and bullets; then we set off again at a fair trot.

17

We were at Vincennes by five to nine.

A carriage arrived at just the same time as ours: it was M. de Château-Renaud's.

We plunged into the wood, each taking a different route. Our coachmen were to join up on the main alley.

A few moments later, we were at the appointed place.

'Gentlemen,' said Louis, getting out first, 'as you know, I have no desire at all to come to terms.'

'But...' I said, going over to him.

'Oh, my dear fellow! Remember that, after the secret with which I have entrusted you, you in particular have no right to suggest or accept any such arrangement.'

I bowed my head to this imperious demand which, for me, represented a last will and testament.

We left Louis near the carriage and walked over to where M. de Boissy and M. de Châteaugrand were standing.

The Baron de Giordano was holding the box of pistols. We exchanged bows.

'Gentlemen,' said the Baron de Giordano, 'in circumstances such as those in which we find ourselves, the shortest compliments are the best; we may be disturbed in our task at any moment. We had promised to bring the weapons, and here they are; please examine them, we have just this minute picked them up from the pistol-maker's, and we give you our word that M. Louis de Franchi has not even seen them.'

'There was absolutely no need for you to insist, Monsieur,' replied the Vicomte de Châteaugrand, 'we know with whom we are dealing.'

And, taking one pistol, while M. de Boissy took the other, the two seconds checked the mechanism and examined the calibre.

'They are ordinary shooting pistols, and they have never been used,' said the Baron; 'now, will the parties be free or not to use the double trigger?'

'My feeling,' said M. de Boissy, 'is that each man must do as he sees best – whatever he is most used to.'

'Very well,' said the Baron de Giordano. 'It is good to have an even playing field.'

'In that case, you can inform Monsieur de Franchi, and we will inform Monsieur de Château-Renaud.'

'Agreed. Now, Monsieur, we have brought the weapons,' continued the Baron de Giordano, 'it is for you to load them.'

The two young men each took one of the pistols, measured out exactly the same amount of gunpowder, took two bullets at random, and thrust them into the barrel with the little mallet.

During this operation, in which I had not wished to participate, I went over to Louis, who received me with a smile on his lips.

'Don't forget any of the things I have asked you to do,' he said. 'You will ensure that Giordano – as I have requested in the letter I have given him – says nothing of this, either to my mother or to my brother. Make sure, too, that the papers don't mention this duel, or, if they do, that they don't give any names.'

'So you are still in thrall to that terrible conviction that the duel will be fatal to you?' I asked.

'I am more convinced of it than ever. But you will do me justice in this at least, won't you? You'll say that I saw death coming like a true Corsican.'

'Your calmness, my dear de Franchi, is so great that it gives me cause to hope that you yourself are not completely convinced.'

Louis took out his watch.

'I still have seven minutes to live,' he said; 'look, here's my watch; keep it, please, as a souvenir of me: it's an excellent Bréguet.'

I took the watch, shaking de Franchi's hand.

'In eight minutes,' I told him, 'I hope to be giving it back to you.'

'Let's say no more of that,' he told me; 'the gentlemen are approaching.'

'Gentlemen,' said the Vicomte de Châteaugrand, 'there ought to be, here on the right, a clearing that I used for my own purposes last year; shall we try to find it? We'll be better off there than in an alley where we might be seen and disturbed.'

'Guide us to the spot, Monsieur,' said the Baron Giordano Martelli; 'we'll follow.'

The Vicomte walked on ahead, and we followed in two separate groups. Soon, we did indeed find ourselves, in about fifteen yards or so, going down an almost imperceptible slope, in the middle of a clearing that had probably once been a pond like that in Auteuil, and was now completely dried up, forming a hollow in the ground surrounded on all sides by a kind of bank; so the terrain seemed to have been purposefully made to act as a theatre for a scene of the kind that was about to happen.

'Monsieur Martelli,' said the Vicomte, 'will you measure out the paces with me?'

The Baron replied with a nod; then, going over to stand next to M. de Châteaugrand, they measured out twenty paces of ordinary length.

So I was left for a few seconds alone with de Franchi.

'By the way,' he said to me, 'you will find my testament on the table where I was writing when you came in.'

'Very well,' I said, 'rest assured I will.'

'Gentlemen, when you are ready,' said the Vicomte de Châteaugrand.

'Here I am,' replied Louis. 'Farewell, my dear friend! Thank you for all the trouble you have taken on my behalf – not to mention,' he added with a melancholy smile, 'all the trouble you will still be put to on my behalf.'

I took his hand; it was cold, but not trembling.

'Come now,' I said, 'forget last night's apparition and just aim as well as you can.'

'Do you remember the *Freischütz*?'[23]

'Yes.'

'Well, as you know, every bullet has its destination… Farewell.'

On his way he crossed the path of Baron Giordano, who was holding the pistol meant for him; he took it, and without even glancing at it, went and took up his place at the spot indicated by a handkerchief.

M. de Château-Renaud was already at his place.

There was a moment of melancholy silence during which the two young men saluted their seconds, then those of their opponent, and finally each other.

M. de Château-Renaud seemed perfectly well used to this kind of duel and he was smiling like a man sure of his skill. Perhaps he also knew that this was the first time that Louis de Franchi had ever held a pistol.

Louis was calm and cold; his handsome head looked like a marble bust.

'Well, gentlemen,' said Château-Renaud, 'as you can see, we are waiting.'

Louis looked at me for one last time; then, with a smile, he raised his eyes to the sky.

'Now then, gentlemen,' said Châteaugrand, 'make ready.'

Then, clapping his hands:

'One… two… three…'

The two shots melded into one explosion.

At the same moment, I saw Louis de Franchi spin round twice and fall to one knee.

M. de Château-Renaud was still standing; only the lapel of his jacket had been pierced.

I dashed over to Louis de Franchi.

'Are you wounded?' I asked him.

He tried to reply, but in vain; a bloody foam appeared on his lips.

At the same time, he dropped the pistol and his hand touched the right side of his chest.

In his jacket there was a tiny hole, barely visible, no bigger than the tip of your small finger.

'Monsieur le Baron,' I cried, 'run to the barracks and fetch the regimental surgeon.'

But de Franchi gathered his strength and motioned with his head to Giordano to indicate that there was no point.

At the same time, he fell onto his other knee.

M. de Château-Renaud immediately walked away; but his two seconds came up to the wounded man.

Meanwhile we had opened his jacket and torn open the waistcoat and shirt.

The bullet had entered beneath the sixth rib on the right and come out just above the left hip.

Every time the dying man breathed out, blood spurted out from the two wounds.

It was clear that the wound was fatal.

'Monsieur de Franchi,' said the Vicomte de Châteaugrand, 'we are most sorry, I can assure you, at the outcome of this unfortunate affair, and we hope that you bear no hatred toward Monsieur de Château-Renaud.'

'Yes, yes…,' murmured the wounded man, 'yes, I forgive him…; but I want him to go away… to go away…'

Then, turning to me with an effort, he said, 'Remember your promise.'

'Oh, I swear it will be carried out just as you desire.'

'And now,' he said with a smile, 'look at your watch.'

And he fell back and breathed his last.

I looked at the watch: it was ten past nine precisely.

Then I turned to look at Louis de Franchi: he was dead.

We took the body back to his home, and, while Baron de Giordano went to register his death at the local police station, I and Joseph carried him up to his room.

The poor servant was weeping bitterly.

When we entered, my eyes involuntarily turned to the clock. It said ten past nine.

They had probably forgotten to wind it up, and it had stopped at just this time.

A moment later, Baron Giordano came back with the police. He had told them what had happened and they had come to seal the room.

The Baron wanted to send letters to the friends and acquaintances of the dead man to inform them of his death; but I asked him first to read the letter that Louis de Franchi had given him when we set off.

This letter contained a sincere request to conceal the cause of his death from Lucien, and asked that the burial be performed without any pomp or ceremony, so that nobody would discover the true circumstances.

Baron Giordano said that he would attend to all these details, and I immediately went off to pay a double visit to MM.

de Boissy and de Châteaugrand, begging them to say nothing of this unfortunate affair, and requesting them to ask M. de Château-Renaud to leave Paris, at least for some time, without telling him the reason why we wished him to absent himself.

They promised me that they would carry out my wishes to the best of their ability, and, while they were on their way to see M. de Château-Renaud, I went to post the letter informing Madame de Franchi that her son had just died of a cerebral fever.

18

Unusually for this sort of affair, the duel roused little comment.

The newspapers themselves, those blaring and false trumpets of publicity, said nothing.

Only a few close friends accompanied the unfortunate young man's body to Père-Lachaise. However, despite the insistent requests made to M. de Château-Renaud, he refused to leave Paris.

I had toyed with the idea of sending a letter to Louis's family, to follow the one he had sent them himself; but although my purpose was of the best, I would have found it abhorrent to lie about the death of a son and a brother: I was convinced that Louis himself had fought against this idea for a long time, and that only the weight of the reasons he had given me had led him to take the course of action he did.

So, at the risk of being accused of indifference or even of ingratitude, I had kept my silence, and Baron Giordano had been obliged to do the same.

Five days after the event, at around eleven in the evening, I was working at my desk, by my fireside, alone, and in a rather glum frame of mind, when my servant came in, closed the door quickly behind him, and – in a rather agitated tone of voice – told me that M. de Franchi had asked to speak to me.

I turned round and stared at him: he was deadly pale.

'What was that you said, Victor?' I asked.

'Oh, Monsieur!' he said, 'to tell you the truth, I really don't know what to say.'

'Which Monsieur de Franchi do you mean? Out with it!'

'I mean... Monsieur's friend... the one I saw coming here on one or two occasions...'

'You are crazy, my dear fellow! Surely you know we had the misfortune to lose him five days ago?'

'Yes, Monsieur; and that is why Monsieur finds me looking so upset. He rang the bell; I was in the antechamber; I went to open the door. As soon as I saw him, I took a step or two back. Then he came in, and asked whether Monsieur was at home; I was so aghast that I answered "yes". Then he told me, "Go and inform him that Monsieur de Franchi is asking to see him." Upon which, here I came.'

'You are crazy, my dear fellow! The antechamber must have been poorly lit and you couldn't see properly; you were still half asleep and didn't hear properly. Go back and ask him to repeat his name.'

'Oh, there is no point in that, I swear to Monsieur that I am not mistaken; I saw and heard correctly.'

'Well, tell him to come.'

Victor turned to the door, trembling all over; I stayed in my room and said, 'Let Monsieur be so kind as to come in.'

Immediately, despite the carpet which muffled them somewhat, I heard footsteps crossing the salon and coming towards my room; then, almost immediately, I did indeed see M. de Franchi appearing at my door.

I have to confess that my first feelings were of terror; I stood up and took a step backwards.

'Forgive me for disturbing you at such an hour,' said M. de Franchi, 'but I arrived ten minutes ago, and you will understand that I did not wish to wait until tomorrow to come and talk with you.'

'Ah, my dear Lucien,' I exclaimed, running over to him and hugging him to my chest, 'it's you, it's really you!'

And a few involuntary tears trickled from my eyes.

'Yes,' he said, 'it's me.'

I calculated the length of time that had elapsed; the letter could hardly have arrived in Ajaccio, let alone Sullacaro.

'Ah, good Lord!' I exclaimed; 'so you can't know what's happened!'

'I know all about it,' he said.

'What? Everything?'

'Yes.'

'Victor,' I said, turning to my valet, who was still extremely uneasy, 'leave us, or rather come back in a quarter of an hour, with a tray of food and drink; you will have supper with me, Lucien, and stay overnight, won't you?'

'I am happy to accept,' he said; 'I haven't eaten since I left Auxerre. Then, as nobody knew me – or rather,' he added, with a smile of profound sadness, 'since everyone seemed to recognise me at the home of my poor brother, they refused to open the door, and I went away, leaving the house in turmoil.'

'Indeed, my dear Lucien, your resemblance with Louis is so close that I myself was struck by it just now.'

'What!' exclaimed Victor, who had still not managed to tear himself away. 'So Monsieur is the brother…?'

'Yes; but go along, get some food ready for us.'

Victor went out. We were alone.

I took Lucien by the hand, led him over to an armchair, and sat down next to him.

'But,' I said, feeling increasingly amazed at his presence, 'you must have already been on your way here when you heard the news of his death?'

'No, I was in Sullacaro.'

'Impossible. Your brother's letter can only just have arrived.'

'You have forgotten Bürger's ballad, my dear Alexandre; "the dead travel fast"!'[24]

I trembled.

'What do you mean? Explain yourself; I don't understand.'

'Have you forgotten what I told you about the apparitions that are a familiar event in our family?'

'So you have seen your brother again?'

'Yes.'

'When was that?'

'During the night of the sixteenth to the seventeenth.'

'And he told you everything?'

'Everything.'

'He told you that he was dead?'

'He told me that he had been killed: once they are dead, people no longer lie.'

'Did he tell you how?'

'In a duel.'

'By whom?'

'By Monsieur de Château-Renaud.'

'No, tell me it's not so… no!' I said. 'You learnt it some other way, didn't you?'

'Do you think I'm in any state of mind to joke?'

'Forgive me. But the fact is that what you are telling me is so strange, and everything that happens to you – to you and your brother – is so far outside the laws of nature…'

'…that you refuse to believe in it, isn't that so? I can understand that! But look,' he said, opening his shirt, and showing me a blue mark imprinted on his skin, above the sixth rib on the right, 'will you believe this?'

'Indeed!' I exclaimed, 'it was just in that place that your brother was hit.'

'And the bullet came out here, didn't it?…' continued Lucien, placing his finger just above his left hip.

'It's a miracle!' I exclaimed.

'And now,' he continued, 'would you like me to tell you what time he died?'

'Tell me!'

'At ten past nine.'

'Look, Lucien, tell me everything, I want to hear it now: I just can't understand things when I have to ask you questions and then listen to your incredible replies. I prefer a proper story.'

19

Lucien propped himself up on one elbow in his armchair, gazed at me fixedly, and continued.

'Oh, good Lord, it's perfectly simple. The day my brother was killed, I'd gone out on horseback early in the morning, and was setting off to see our shepherds near Carboni. I'd just looked to see what time it was and was putting my watch back in its fob when I felt such a violent pain in my side that I fainted. When I opened my eyes again, I was lying on the ground in Orlandini's arms – he was throwing water into my face. My horse was right nearby, prodding its nose at me, sniffing and snorting.

'"Well," said Orlandini, "whatever has happened to you?"

'"Good Lord," I replied, "I really don't know myself; but didn't you just hear a rifle shot?"

'"No."

'"I think I've just been hit, here."

'And I showed him the place where I was feeling pain.

'"To begin with," he replied, "there wasn't any rifle or pistol shot; and secondly, there's no hole in your frock coat."

'"In that case," I said, "it's my brother; he's just been killed."

'"Ah!" he said. "That's a different matter."

'I opened my coat and found the mark I showed you just now; but, at first glance, it looked sore and seemed to be bleeding.

'For a moment, I felt so overcome by this double pain, physical and psychological, that I was tempted to go back to Sullacaro; but I thought of my mother: she wasn't expecting me until supper time, so I would have to think of some reason for my return, and I had no reason I could give her.

'In addition, I didn't want to inform her that my brother was dead without being fully certain of the facts.

'So I continued on my way, and didn't return home until six in the evening.

'My poor mother greeted me as usual; it was evident that she didn't suspect a thing.

'Straight away after supper, I went back up to my room.

'As I was walking along the corridor that you will remember, the wind blew out my candle.

'I was just about to go downstairs to relight it when, through the chink under the door, I saw there was a light in my brother's room.

'I thought that Griffo must have been in the room for some reason or other and had forgotten to take his lamp.

'I pushed open the door; a candle was burning near my brother's bed and on that same bed lay my brother, naked and bleeding.

'I must confess that I stood there for a moment, rooted to the spot with terror; then I went over to him.

'I touched him… He was already cold.

'The bullet had gone straight through him, at the same place where I had felt the shot, and a few drops of blood were falling from the scarlet lips of the wound.

'It was clear to me that my brother had been killed.

'I fell to my knees and, leaning my head against the bed, closed my eyes and started to pray.

'When I reopened them, I was in the deepest darkness; the candle had gone out and the vision had disappeared.

'I felt around on the bed; it was empty.

'Listen: I have to confess that I think I'm as brave as any man, but when I came out of the room, feeling my way, the hair on the back of my head was standing up and my brow was covered in sweat.

'I went down to get another candle; my mother saw me and uttered a cry.

'"Whatever's the matter?" she said, "and why are you so pale?"

'"There's nothing the matter," I replied.

'And, picking up another candle, I went back upstairs.

'This time, the candle didn't go out, and I went into my brother's room... It was empty.

'The candle had completely vanished: nothing had been on the mattress to leave the imprint of its weight.

'On the floor lay my first candle; I relit it.

'In spite of the absence of any new conclusive evidence, I had seen enough to be convinced.

'At ten past nine in the morning, my brother had been killed. I returned to my room and went to bed, my mind in turmoil.

'As you can imagine, I took a long time to get to sleep; finally, my weariness won out over my turmoil, and sleep overcame me.

'Then everything proceeded as in the shape of a dream; I saw just how the events had occurred; I saw the man who killed him; I heard his name being uttered: he is Monsieur de Château-Renaud.'

'Alas, all that is perfectly true,' I replied. 'But why have you come to Paris?'

'I have come to kill the man who killed my brother.'

'Kill him...?'

'Oh, don't worry – not in the Corsican way, behind a hedge or from behind a wall: no, no, in the French manner, with white gloves, a jabot, and lace cuffs.'

'And does Madame de Franchi know that you came to Paris with this in mind?'

'Yes.'

'And she allowed you to leave?'

'She kissed me on my forehead and said, "Go!" My mother is a true Corsican.'

'And so you have come!'

'Here I am.'

'But, while he was still alive, your brother didn't want to be avenged.'

'Well,' said Lucien, with a bitter smile, 'he must have changed his mind since dying.'

Just then, the valet came in carrying our supper: we sat down at table.

Lucien ate like a man whose mind is free from worries.

After supper, I took him to his room. He thanked me, shook me by the hand, and wished me a good night.

He showed the calm that, in strong and brave souls, follows a decision made with unshakeable resolve.

The next day, he came into my room as soon as my servant told him I was dressed and ready.

'Will you come with me to Vincennes?' he asked. 'It's a pious pilgrimage that I intend to perform; if you don't have the time, I'll go by myself.'

'What do you mean – alone? Who'll show you where it happened?'

'Oh, I'll easily recognise it; didn't I tell you that I saw it in a dream?'

I was curious to know how far this strange intuition of his would go.

'Fine then, I'll come with you,' I said.

'Very well, you can get ready while I'm writing to Giordano.

You'll allow me to make use of your valet to take a letter, won't you?'

'He is at your disposal.'

'Thank you.'

He went out and came back ten minutes later with his letter, which he handed over to my servant.

I had been out to hire a cabriolet; we got in, and set off for Vincennes.

When we reached the crossroads, Lucien said, 'We're nearly there, aren't we?'

'Yes, fifteen yards or so from here, we'll be at the spot where we entered the forest.'

'It's here!' said the young man, asking the cabriolet to halt.

It was the very spot.

Lucien walked unhesitatingly into the wood, just as if he had been here a score of times already. He walked straight to the hollow in the ground, and, when he reached it, paused to get his bearings. Then he walked to the place where his brother had fallen, bent over the ground, and saw a reddish stain on the earth.

'This is it,' he said.

Then he slowly lowered his head and kissed the grassy spot.

Then, his eyes aflame, he straightened up and walked across the full length of the hollow to reach the spot from which M. de Château-Renaud had fired.

'This was where he was,' he said, tapping with his foot; 'this is where you will see him tomorrow, lying prostrate.'

'What?' I said. 'Tomorrow?'

'Yes. Either he is a coward, or, tomorrow, he will grant me my revenge.'

'But, my dear Lucien,' I said, 'as you know, it is our habit in France to consider that a duel entails no consequences other than the natural consequences of that duel. Monsieur de Château-Renaud fought a duel with your brother, whom he had challenged to a duel, but he has no quarrel with you.'

'Ah, I see. So, in your view, Monsieur de Château-Renaud had the right to challenge my brother, because my brother had offered his protection to a woman whom that man had cravenly betrayed. Monsieur de Château-Renaud killed my brother, who had never touched a pistol; he killed him with as little risk to himself as if he had been firing at that roebuck looking at us over there – and *I* do not have any right to challenge Monsieur de Château-Renaud? Come now!'

I lowered my eyes and said nothing.

'In any case,' he continued, 'you have no reason to get involved in any of this. Rest assured: I wrote to Giordano this morning and, by the time we return to Paris, it will all be arranged. Do you really think Monsieur de Château-Renaud will reject my proposal?'

'Unfortunately, Monsieur de Château-Renaud has a reputation for bravery that, I have to confess, leaves me not the slightest doubts about his reply.'

'Well then, everything is perfect,' said Lucien. 'Let's go and have lunch.'

We returned to the alley and got back into the cabriolet.

'Coachman,' I said, 'rue de Rivoli.'

'No,' said Lucien, 'I'm inviting you out for lunch. Coachman, the Café de Paris. Isn't that where my brother used to dine?'

'I believe so.'

'Anyway, that's where I've agreed to meet Giordano.'

'Very well: the Café de Paris.'

Half an hour later, we were at the restaurant door.

20

Lucien's entry into the restaurant was yet one more proof of the strange resemblance between himself and his brother.

The news of Louis's death had spread, perhaps not in all its details, admittedly, but spread it had, and the sudden appearance of Lucien seemed to dumbfound everyone present.

I asked for a private room, in view of the fact that the Baron Giordano would be joining us.

So we were given the room at the back.

Lucien started to read the newspapers with an icy calm that resembled rank insensitivity.

Halfway through the meal, Giordano came in.

The two young men had not seen each other for four or five years, but a handshake was the only sign of friendship they vouchsafed each other.

'Well,' he said, 'it's all arranged.'

'Has Monsieur de Château-Renaud accepted?'

'Yes, but on one condition: that after you, everyone will leave him alone.'

'Oh, he can be sure of that: I am the last of the de Franchi. Did you see him in person, or was it his seconds?'

'Himself. He has agreed to inform Messieurs de Boissy and de Châteaugrand. As for the weapons, the time and the place, they will all be the same.'

'Excellent… Take a seat, and have some lunch.'

The Baron sat down, and we talked about other things.

After lunch, Lucien asked us to have him officially recognised by the police inspector who had sealed the room, and by the proprietor of the house where his brother lived. He wanted to spend this last night that lay between himself and vengeance in Louis's very own room.

All this official activity filled a good part of the day, and it wasn't until around five in the evening that Lucien could enter his brother's apartment. We left him alone; sorrow has a sense of privacy that must be respected.

Lucien arranged to meet us the next day at eight o'clock. He asked me to try and get the same pistols, and indeed to buy them, if they were for sale.

So I immediately went to Devisme's, and purchased the pistols for six hundred francs. The next day, at a quarter to eight, I was at Lucien's.

When I went in, he was sitting in the same place and writing at the same table where I had found his brother busy writing. He had a smile on his lips, though he was deadly pale.

'Good day,' he said to me. 'I'm writing to my mother.'

'I hope that you have less unhappy news to give her than the news your brother sent her, a week ago today.'

'I am telling her that she can pray for her son in all tranquillity: he has been avenged.'

'How can you be so certain?'

'Hadn't my brother foretold his own death to you? Well, I am foretelling the death of Monsieur de Château-Renaud to you.'

He rose and, touching me on the temple, said, 'There – that's where I'll put my bullet.'

'And you?'

'He won't even touch me!'

'But at least wait until the outcome of the duel has been decided before sending the letter.'

'There's absolutely no point.'

He rang. The valet appeared.

'Joseph,' he said, 'take this letter to the post office.'

'But have you seen your brother again?'

'Yes,' he replied.

How strange it all was, these two duels, one after the other, in which one of the two adversaries was condemned in advance to die. Just at that moment, Baron Giordano arrived. It was eight o'clock. We set off.

Lucien was in such a hurry to arrive, and drove the coachman on so vehemently, that we were at the meeting place ten minutes before the hour.

Our opponents arrived at nine o'clock precisely. They were all three on horseback and followed by a servant, also on horseback.

M. de Château-Renaud had his hand inside his jacket, and at first I thought his arm must be in a sling.

Fifteen yards or so away from us, those gentlemen dismounted and threw the bridles of their horses to their servants.

M. de Château-Renaud stayed in the background, but he did glance at Lucien; although he was some way away from us, I could see him going pale. He turned round and, with the whip he was carrying in his left hand, passed the time flicking the little flowers that grew amid the grass.

'Here we are, gentlemen,' said MM. de Châteaugrand and de Boissy. 'But you know our conditions: this duel is to be the last and, whatever its outcome, Monsieur de Château-Renaud will need answer to nobody else for the twofold result.'

'Agreed,' Giordano and I both replied.

Lucien gave a short bow to signal his assent.

'You have weapons, Messieurs?' asked the Vicomte de Châteaugrand.

'The same.'

'And Monsieur de Franchi is quite unfamiliar with them.'

'He is even less familiar with them than is Monsieur de Château-Renaud. Monsieur de Château-Renaud has used them once. Monsieur de Franchi has not seen them yet.'

'Very good, Messieurs. Come, Château-Renaud.'

Immediately we plunged into the wood without uttering a single word: each of us had hardly recovered from the events the scene of which we were about to revisit, and each of us sensed that something no less terrible was about to happen.

We arrived at the hollow in the ground.

M. de Château-Renaud seemed calm, thanks to his enormous self-control; but those who had seen him in these two encounters could notice an appreciable difference.

From time to time, he cast a furtive glance at Lucien, and this glance expressed a disquiet bordering on real fear.

Perhaps it was the close resemblance of the two brothers that preoccupied him, and perhaps he saw in Lucien the avenging shade of Louis.

While the pistols were being loaded, I finally saw him pull his hand from his frock coat; his hand was wrapped in a damp handkerchief that was clearly meant to prevent it trembling feverishly.

Lucien waited, his eye calm and steady, like that of a man sure of his revenge.

Without anyone pointing out his place to him, Lucien went and stood in the same spot as his brother had done; this naturally forced M. de Château-Renaud to go to the spot that he, too, had earlier occupied.

Lucien took possession of his weapon with a smile of joy.

As M. de Château-Renaud took his weapon in turn, his pallor turned to an intense whiteness. Then he passed his hand between his cravat and his neck as if his cravat were choking him.

Nobody can imagine the feeling of involuntary terror that filled me as I gazed at this young man – handsome, rich, elegant – who, the day before, had still imagined he had long years of life ahead of him and who now, with sweat on his brow and anguish in his heart, sensed that he was condemned to death.

'Are you ready, gentlemen?' asked M. de Châteaugrand.

'Yes,' replied Lucien.

M. de Château-Renaud nodded.

But I did not have the strength to watch, and turned away.

I heard the two handclaps and, at the third, the sound of two pistols going off.

I turned back.

M. de Château-Renaud was lying on the ground, killed outright; he hadn't even uttered a sign or made a single movement.

I went over to the body, impelled by the unassuageable curiosity that leads you to follow a catastrophe to its bitter end; the bullet had gone in through the temple, at the very same place Lucien had indicated.

I ran over to him; he had remained calm and motionless; but when he saw me within reach, he dropped his pistol and flung himself into my arms.

'Oh, my brother! My poor brother!' he cried. And he burst into tears. They were the first tears this young man had ever shed.

NOTES

1. Prospero and Nautilus were celebrated racehorses of the 1830s and 1840s.

2. Jacques Balmat (1762–1834), an Italian mountain guide and the first person (with Michel-Gabriel Paccard) to climb Mont Blanc in 1786. Jean Baptiste Auriol (c.1800–81) was a celebrated circus clown and acrobat.

3. Louis Godefroy Jadin (1805–82) was a painter of animals and landscapes, and a friend and travelling companion of Dumas's.

4. The maquis is the scrubland characteristic of central Corsica (and of much of the south of France).

5. He was actually thirty-eight.

6. Most of these names are still familiar. The less familiar include François-Eudes de Mézeray (1610–83), who wrote a celebrated history of France; Augustin Thierry (1795–1856), who specialised in the history of the Norman Conquest of England and the Merovingian dynasty; François Sulpice Beudant (1787–1850), a geologist and mineralogist; and Léonce Elie de Beaumont (1798–1874), also a geologist.

7. Dumas composed several volumes entitled *Impressions de voyage*. It is interesting that he here classifies them as 'novels'.

8. Sampietro Bastelica, known as Sampieru Corsu (1498–1567), was a Corsican soldier of fortune. He became Lord of Ornano after his marriage to Vanina (or Vannina) d'Ornano. In 1553 he fought for the French against the Genoese during an expedition to Corsica. He personally strangled his wife for treachery (she had been corrupted by a spy from Genoa while her husband was in Istanbul): their story has occasionally been regarded as the inspiration for Shakespeare's *Othello*.

9. Pasquale Paoli (1725–1807), one of Boswell's heroes, fought for Corsican independence.

10. The Battle of Zama (202 BC) was fought between the Romans and the Carthaginians. The latter, led by Hannibal, lost.

11. In Mérimée's *Colomba*, the bandit's name is Brando Savelli.

12. Anton Pietro Filippini (b. c.1530) wrote an *Istoria di Corsica* (1594).

13. Hugo's *Orientales* (1829) is a collection of poems set in visionary landscapes inspired by North Africa and the Middle East. '*Le Feu du ciel*' ('Fire from Heaven') reworks the story of Sodom and Gomorrah.

14. Dumas's father actually died in 1806.

15. Humann was a fashionable tailor of Dumas's day; Boivin and Roussaux, on the following page, were glove-makers of repute.

16. Louis Auguste de Bourbon, duc du Maine (1670–1736), was a bastard (but legitimised) son of Louis XIV. He achieved a degree of political power, but was marginalised by the other French nobles during the Regency.

17. This street is in the Opera district of Paris: in his memoirs, Dumas refers to it as being particularly fashionable.

18. *Mi-carême* marks the halfway point in Lent: the Thursday of the third full week of the forty days of penitence. On this Thursday, the austerities of Lent were relaxed – hence the ball at the Paris Opera.

19. *Les Trois Frères Provençaux* was a famous Paris restaurant.

20. Augustin Grisier (1791–1865) was Dumas's own fencing master. He had also taught fencing to the Russian poet Pushkin (who was killed in a pistol duel).

21. Joseph Méry (1798–1866) was a writer and librettist of the Romantic school.

22. Louis-François Devisme (1806–73) was a well-known maker of pistols.

23. Weber's opera *Der Freischütz* (1821) was based on an old legend in which the Devil offers to a marksman, in return for his soul, a number of bullets that will always reach their target; the Devil keeps one extra bullet that will hit a target of his own choosing.

24. Gottfried Bürger's macabre ballad *Lenore* (1773) includes the words '*Denn die Todten reiten schnell*' ('For the dead ride fast').

BIOGRAPHICAL NOTE

Alexandre Dumas was born in Villes-Cotterêts, France, in 1802. His father, a general in Napoleon's army, died when Dumas was not yet four years old, leaving the family impoverished.

In 1823 Dumas moved to Paris in order to find work. He was given a position with the duc d'Orléans (later King Louis-Philippe), and supplemented his income by working in the theatre and in publishing. He began writing plays, eventually finding success with a production of his play *Henri III et sa cour* [*Henry III and his Court*] in 1829. This he followed up with *La Tour de Nesle* [*The Tower of Nesle*] (1832), which is considered one of the great masterpieces of French melodrama. Alongside his plays, Dumas also penned novels and short stories; his output was prodigious and he produced some two hundred and fifty works. His historical novels were then, as now, his most popular creations, and he is recognised as playing an important role in the development of the genre. Among his most famous historical novels are *Les trois mousquetaires* [*The Three Musketeers*] (1844) and *Le Comte de Monte-Cristo* [*The Count of Monte Cristo*] (1844–5).

Dumas took considerable interest in the politics of his day, and was involved in the revolution of July 1830. In 1858 he travelled to Russia, and then, in 1860, to Italy, where he supported Garibaldi and the Italian Risorgimento. He lived an extravagant lifestyle, showering money on mistresses and friends, and soon found himself in considerable debt. He had married in 1840 – having previously fathered an illegitimate son, Alexandre Dumas *fils*, in 1824 – but he whittled away his wife's dowry so rapidly that the marriage proved short lived.

Dumas died from a stroke in December 1870. His son went on to become an author in his own right, but he refrained from his father's lifestyle of excess.

Andrew Brown studied at the University of Cambridge, where he taught French for many years. He now works as a freelance teacher and translator. He is the author of *Roland Barthes: The Figures of Writing* (OUP, 1993), and his translations include *Memoirs of a Madman* by Gustave Flaubert, *For a Night of Love* by Emile Zola, *The Jinx* by Théophile Gautier, *Mademoiselle de Scudéri* by E.T.A. Hoffmann, *Theseus* by André Gide, *Incest* by Marquis de Sade, *The Ghost-seer* by Friedrich von Schiller, *Colonel Chabert* by Honoré de Balzac, *Memoirs of an Egotist* by Stendhal, *Butterball* by Guy de Maupassant and *With the Flow* by Joris-Karl Huysmans, all published by Hesperus Press.